D0094751

PS
3604
I48
K

THE

KRZYZEWSKIVILLE

TALES

THE
Krzyzewskiville
TALES

AARON DININ

With a foreword by Mickie Krzyzewski

DUKE UNIVERSITY PRESS

Durham and London

2005

© 2005 Duke University Press
All rights reserved
Printed in the United States of
America on acid-free paper ∞
Typeset in Adobe Jenson by
Tseng Information Systems
Library of Congress Cataloging-
in-Publication Data appear on
the last printed page
of this book.

*Duke University Press
gratefully acknowledges the
support of the Duke University
Stores, which provided funds
toward the production
of this book.*

For my father, Lenny,
whose love and untiring support
have allowed me
to accomplish my dreams

CONTENTS

FOREWORD

Standing here in my husband's office on the sixth floor of the Schwartz-Butters building and looking out over the tent city that appears like a vision every year, my feeling of amusement quickly turns to an indescribable sense of pride. Pride in my husband, Coach K; pride in the accomplishments of our team; pride in Duke University and a newfound pride in the students who occupy the tents in Krzyzewskiville. My pride in the students is newly found because I learned so much about them and Krzyzewskiville from the pages of this book. Although I have always known that we need our "sixth man" and that they are a big part of our team, until reading *The Krzyzewskiville Tales*, I did not realize how much I respect them. They "get it." They understand that basketball at Duke evolved into a special culture and that they are members of that culture. The love, commitment, and ownership that is felt by this unique group of students for their school and team is not something that happens just anywhere. It takes great effort to be able to create the spirit that lives in Krzyzewskiville. That spirit is nourished by living together in self-imposed sacrifice for the good of a single common cause. That spirit strengthens and grows and spreads and becomes an entity that defies definition. *The Krzyzewskiville Tales* gives insight into that entity. Is it mythical? Is it magical? Is it insanity? Is it right? Yes. — Mickie K

PREFACE

The following tales were inspired by Geoffrey Chaucer's verse poem *The Canterbury Tales*, and, of course, the students of Duke University and their adventures in Krzyzewskiville. Since the inception of this project, and through its various stages of writings and rewritings, revisions and re-revisions, I have often taken a moment to pause and reflect on what Mr. Chaucer might think. What would he say if he knew that his famous storyline was, hundreds of years later, plundered for a book about the quirky sports tradition of a few overzealous college kids? My first instinct is to hope that he might be flattered; after all, as the saying goes, imitation is the sincerest form of flattery. More important, I think Chaucer would wonder *why* I chose his model of storytelling pilgrims on their trek to a religious shrine as the foundation for a story about Krzyzewskiville. To curious readers asking the same question I imagine Geoffrey Chaucer might let me offer my thoughts and, in the process, I hope, provide an answer or two.

The original intent of this project on Krzyzewskiville was to organize the tradition's basic, chronological history. I had hoped, through mostly archival research, to be able to lay out an ordered timeline of K-ville; but once I began the search for physical records of Krzyzewskiville and tenting at Duke, I discovered that few of K-ville's factual events have been recorded. The documents I discovered consisted for the most part of old newspaper clippings providing a broad overview of tenting or offering an argument for or against a particular aspect of the system. Detailed records of historical events do not exist.

Because physical records cannot be consulted, the next logical step was to go straight to the participants of K-ville and ask them for their accounts. Finding former tenters to discuss their K-ville experiences was an easy task: they love nothing more than to relate their memories of tenting to current students. My discussion of the intricacies of a particular drinking game with a thirty-five-year-old executive in a pinstriped suit is an experience I think only K-ville could have initiated. To these many people—lawyers, doctors, teachers, businessmen, and others —for the hours spent telling me your tales I cannot thank you enough. But the many former tenters who offered their stories should know that not one of them supplied the same account of any particular event. Instead of solidifying my information regarding the history of Krzyzewskiville, the alumni interviews only muddled the picture. No two storytellers gave the same account, and none of their accounts matched up with the few available written versions. As my research progressed, the only aspect of K-ville that was becoming clear was that the passing of time tends to cause an exaggeration of the events therein.

Any hopes of composing a chronological history of Krzyzewskiville had vanished by the fifth or sixth interview; extracting the true events from the stories would have been impossible.

But all the interviewees had something in common (besides utter inconsistency): when I spoke with them, they each became storytellers. They all relished the opportunity to tell their tales of tenting. On that realization, the link to *The Canterbury Tales* started to take form in my mind. I began to conceive of a model for the different stories which posed them as fiction (a nod to their potentially tenuous ties to true fact) but allowed them to work within the context of the historical events. What better way to accomplish this task than to have the storytellers I had met become the model for the storytellers in the book? And if those K-ville storytellers were to be modeled on Chaucer's storytelling pilgrims, what would inspire them to sit around and tell stories? Why not have a storytelling competition?

Any reader who has experienced a night of personal checks in Krzyzewskiville might ask himself, Would a group of students actually sit down and tell stories about K-ville while 1,200 screaming, laughing, and often drunk college kids run around nearby? That, of course, doesn't really happen . . . or at least it hasn't in my experience. Granted, a few stories have been passed along over the years, but never in such detail and never in such a setting. However, I'll ask my readers to suspend disbelief for a few pages in the interest of a good story — or twelve.

The advantages of using *The Canterbury Tales* as my model for this book extend beyond the convenience of structure. The tale of a religion major will hit on this particular point in a little more depth, but for now, I should compare the journeys described in the two volumes. Chaucer's characters are a group of companions on a religious pilgrimage. An argument for a relationship between basketball at Duke and religion is one I will save for a later date (and perhaps I will pose it to a psychology major instead of an English major), but suffice it to say that the parallels are eerily similar. These Krzyzewskiville tenters are, in their own right, on a quasi-religious pilgrimage. Tenting is their trip, and Cameron is their holy destination. Chaucer offers us a diverse group of pilgrims, giving his readers a range of social gestures and points of view. Likewise, a tent in K-ville can often bring together a diverse group of students with varying social, economic, and educational backgrounds. My hope is to give the reader the sense of how these unlikely groups of friends might interact. What happens when you put an engineering student with a history major? How will their stories and preoccupations differ?

Yet, as much as Chaucer's work provides a basic structure for my own, and although there may be similarities between our tales, I would be remiss if I did not acknowledge our differing tasks. To any teacher reading these tales who has ever taught me something of Chaucer and his works, I promise I paid attention in your class. Please do not assume the variances to be misunderstandings of the text but instead alterations of necessity. The most obvious difference between the two volumes comes in their language and format: Chaucer's work appears in Middle English verse, mine in contemporary English prose. Not only would the use of verse be impractical, but it might also hinder the reader's experience. In addition to the obvious

Students wander Krzyzewskiville at night.

Duke Indoor Stadium
(Cameron) under construction, 1940.

Crowd Shot of Duke Indoor Stadium
(Cameron) during inaugural season, 1940.

Art Heyman, 1963 National Player of the Year.

Johnny Dawkins (center,
dunking), 1986 National Player of the Year.

First official Krzyzewskiville, 1986.

A student does his homework on a laptop
while waiting in his tent.

COURTESY OF DUKE UNIVERSITY PHOTOGRAPHY.

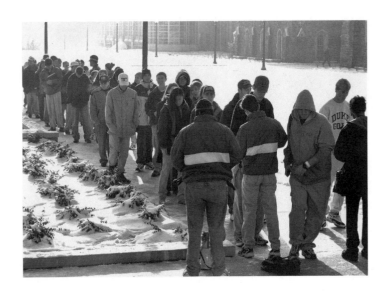

Despite the snow, students wait in line as line monitors
distribute wristbands to the upcoming game later that day.

A group of Cameron Crazies prepare themselves for a game.

The Crazies cheer on Duke's team together in
Cameron during the 2001 national championship game.

The sign that officially labels the tent city
as Krzyzewskiville is presented to Coach K.

This sign outside of Krzyzewskiville
points the way to Indianapolis (the site of the
Final Four that year), and "Chapel Hell."

Students socialize in Krzyzewskiville while
waiting for a personal check to be called.

The Krzyzewskiville sign labels the tent city;
behind it is Tent 15, which also happens to be the jersey
number of Duke point guard Sean Dockery.

A Cameron Crazie celebrates with his
friends during personal checks.

Basketball players Shavlik Randolph (left), Sean
Dockery (center), and Luol Deng (right) spend time
with their fellow students in Krzyzewskiville.

Basketball player Sean Dockery takes a shot
during a shooting competition in Krzyzewskiville
the night before the UNC game.

Tent 87 has relocated its living room, moving it out
to Krzyzewskiville during personal checks.

Krzyzewskiville after a night of personal checks that saw 1,500 students.

Sign from first official Krzyzewskiville explaining the purpose
of the tents and claiming spots in line, 1986.

difference in style, Chaucer's tales were never completed. With far fewer characters, and far fewer stories to tell, my storytelling competition comes to an end. The question of whether or not my ending is similar to what Chaucer had in mind for his own book can never be answered.

Other differences concern the storytellers' subject matter. All the stories herein focus on one subject, K-ville, whereas the pilgrims in Chaucer's poem had no such constraints. In addition, I have taken up the dual purpose of telling a particular set of stories while attempting to outline a specific history. As a result, I must, to some extent, be true to certain facts of Krzyzewskiville. That said, however, readers should note that this is still a work of fiction. Although many of the events discussed herein did occur, names have been changed and characters added or removed to fit my purposes and my story. K-ville is, in many respects, a city, and it would be impossible for me to witness, discuss, or record every event that has taken place within its borders. Often, in order to incorporate more information, stories have been combined. This was not done to undermine what factual knowledge we do have of K-ville, but rather to allow the reader to come away with a better sense of what Krzyzewskiville is. The tenting tradition doesn't make much sense, but it happens year after year. If I have done my job well, by the end of these pages, you will have a better understanding of not only why K-ville exists, but also why it is important.

The following pages are, as the title suggests, tales of Krzyzewskiville. Basketball did indeed motivate the creation of

K-ville, but K-ville is not just about basketball. The intention of this book is not to provide game synopses and player stats; although they occasionally appear, they do not dominate the stories. These are the tales of life in the tenting village. The stories are meant not to laud an already highly praised basketball program, but to reflect the experience of tenting. Indeed, although the Cameron Crazies are discussed, and a tenter is necessarily also a Crazie, *The Krzyzewskiville Tales* are not designed to convey the antics of the student section inside Cameron. The following pages focus on the lawn outside the stadium where attending a basketball game might be the ultimate goal but day-to-day living is the main experience.

For readers who are not veteran tenters or are not fluent in Krzyzewskiville lingo, at the end of this book is Crazie Talk, a glossary of tenting terms. Although I try to explain any stray terms, one or two might have slipped through unexplained. If you encounter such a term or phrase, then feel free to turn to the glossary for clarification.

I now offer these stories of being a Duke student, being a tenter, and most importantly, being a fan. A fan is what I am proud to be, and it is as such that I offer these tales to my fellow fans. May they only add to your personal experiences of supporting your favorite team. Go Devils!

ACKNOWLEDGMENTS

his book has not been without its supporters from the first pitch of the idea. In general, I have to begin by thanking all the Cameron Crazies — past, present, and future. This book is really for you. I've also had the opportunity to meet many people associated with K-villes past. Their names are too numerous to list here, but to all of them I offer my utmost gratitude. Thanks for sharing your stories.

Although I suppose it matters little to him, I believe a thank you is in order to Geoffrey Chaucer.

I would also like to thank Mike Cragg, the assistant athletics director and the director of the Duke Basketball Legacy Fund, for the unending string of answers to my unending string of questions.

The images in this book appear courtesy of the Duke University Archives, thanks to the efforts of the archivists Tim Pyatt and Thomas Harkins, and courtesy of Duke Photography, with additional assistance from Tommy Newnam. I also thank Dean Mary Nijhout and the Duke Undergraduate Research Support program for providing funding for these images.

Thanks to Marianna Torgovnick, a professor in Duke's English department, who has helped me through countless aspects of the process.

A thanks goes out to all of my family, but especially to my mother, Denise, and to my stepmother, Ronnie, who each spent numerous hours reading or listening to my stories of this quirky tenting tradition and offering most helpful advice.

And finally, I would like to acknowledge the incredible work of my editor at Duke University Press, Miriam Angress. I doubt that I taught her half as much about tenting as she has taught me about writing.

THE

KRZYZEWSKIVILLE

TALES

When January with his show'rs frozen
Has shrouded all in this town of Durham,
And coated every bough in shimmering ice
That carves the sun into a thousand lights;
When interrupted are the shortened days
By lengthened nights and gray clouds shading rays
Sent to thaw fingers of an ungloved hand,
And on tree limbs no birds for months will land,
And air suffocates in their brief absence;
Then out come Duke's students to pitch their tents.

GENERAL PROLOGUE

HERE BEGINS THE BOOK OF THE
TALES OF KRZYZEWSKIVILLE

Winter is a season symbolized with splendid whites, but its nights reveal a darker side. The wind sings in steady gusts while the earth rolls on its poles to the East. But the reflective white of a new snow and the engulfing black of the year's longest night can be combined with a proud warrior's courageous blue to represent the insignia of this school. You will encounter a group of winter's most dedicated and storied youths, draped in these three colors: blue, black, and white. Year after year they return to a familiar place of epic fanfare and lonesome waits. The spot is little more than a patch of grass, but from its fertile soil a city annually sprouts.

In this winter season and on this freezing day, I write to you from that city, Krzyzewskiville, as I lie alone in my tent, wrapped in layers of clothing and blankets. The only parts of my body exposed to the numbing air are my stiff fingertips. They roam the cold plastic of the keyboard on my laptop, clumsily pecking out sentences. Because of their sacrifice I can now recount for you the story of this evening's events.

My tent shift began at seven o'clock. On all other Tuesdays, it had ended at nine. The Carolina game would take place tomorrow night, however, and a round of personal checks would be called this evening. For those unfamiliar with the intricacies of the tenting tradition surrounding Duke students' admission into home basketball games, allow me to explain. Five *personal checks* are held over the course of two successive nights. The window during which checks can be called begins at nine o'clock on each of the two nights, with a grace period during the day in between (during which one person from each tent must remain in line), and ends once the fifth and final check is called. All tenters must present themselves at three of these five checks to secure a place in line for admittance to the upcoming game. Only two personal checks had been called last night, which means every tenter will come out to K-ville at some point this evening to make a third check.

Since the hour was nearing nine o'clock on the second night of personal checks, Krzyzewskiville would soon be refilling with students. I lay alone in Tent 25 while a cold rain thudded softly against the canvas roof. I was happy to have some shelter; nylon though it may have been, at least it was waterproof. Not wanting to lose the warmth from the sleeping bags I lay under — and there were many — I remained motionless and awaited the arrival of my fellow students and friends. I have spent many similar hours since our tent was first erected over a month ago. Since then eleven companions and I have taken our turns in Tent 25, dividing our wait in line as we made our yearly pilgrimage through the hallowed lands of that famed tent village named for Duke basketball's illustrious leader, the head coach Michael Krzyzewski. I recognize that these moments of blissful solitude and reflection are rare in college; once more than a thousand undergraduates gathered on this lawn, the silence was sure to be broken. So I endeavored to enjoy the few moments of quiet.

Tonight brought the final test for all twelve of us in Tent 25. We awaited our final personal check. Last night we had all made both checks. One more check for each of us would ensure our tent's place in line for that coveted prize—admittance to Cameron Indoor Stadium and a seat for the marquee matchup with our detested rival from eight miles down the street in Chapel Hill.

My companions began to arrive as nine o'clock still neared. The crescendo of approaching footsteps announced the earliest person's coming. When the steps subsided, a rustle of mesh followed. The blue tent flap drew away, and from the pale orange lamplight outside I could distinguish the face of the first member of my tent to join me for the night. He is a senior and a history major, though I think sports are his greatest passion. Tall but graceful, his build and athleticism help him excel in almost every athletic competition. Of the many he plays, basketball is his favorite, although I am unsure whether that was the case before he arrived in Durham. When not watching Duke games either on television or on the court, he often can be found in the gym. His presence in pickup games seems practically constant, and whichever team he is on is often ensured of a win. Recreating unforgettable moments in Duke basketball history has become his favorite pastime on the hardwood—maybe a Jason Williams behind-the-back pass to Carlos Boozer as he cuts between three defenders. Or perhaps he might reenact Grant Hill's historic near-court-length hurl to Christian Laettner, the play that culminated in the overtime, buzzer-beating shot to defeat Kentucky in the 1992 Eastern regional finals of the NCAA tournament, sending Duke on to its second consecutive national championship.

Not only was this student the first member of my tent to join me, he also held the position and responsibility of the Captain of Tent 25. As a seasoned veteran of the trials of the tenting life, this senior knew how to surmount the animosity tenting can create. Trying to divide a month spent in a tent equally among twelve people leads to trouble—even for the closest of friends. The challenge is even greater when that month is January. Arguments and anger erupt when a tent member fails to bear his or her share of the burden. Some tenters complain about having to spend a Friday night alone in the numbing cold, and others are disgruntled when problems arise with such issues as sanitation or tent maintenance. And, of course, the erratic winter weather can inspire still more resentment.

Theoretically, the job of a captain is not to patrol a tent. Relative to those of his tent mates, a captain's only additional tasks are to register his group and to be in touch with the head line monitor in the event of a missed check. However, our Captain's experience helped him to maintain order when events occurred that might have otherwise led to arguments and conflict within our tent.

Our Captain slipped off his well-worn basketball shoes before entering the tent and set them underneath the overhang outside the entrance. As he ducked his head beneath the flap, he gently cleared his throat and asked, "Aaron, did someone steal your shoes? I don't see them outside." I rolled my eyes and sent a heavy sigh out of the corner of my lips before struggling like a moth from my cocoon of sleeping bags. Once I freed myself I stood upright in the tent next to the Captain who, because of his height, was forced to stand with his head bent to the left. His eyes darted to the scuffed black boots on my feet. As I bent down to untie the laces I answered, "Sorry, my toes had gone numb. But don't worry, I was careful not to rip your precious tent." He didn't acknowledge my snide remark, but instead sat on one of the sleeping bags at the back of the tent. I leaned out the tent's still-open flap to place my shoes next to his on the sidewalk.

When I peered out into the night, I saw, as I had suspected, that the Captain was not alone. With him, as always, was his eager younger brother, a freshman, who, since he mimics his brother's every action, would probably follow the academic path of his older sibling and major in history as well. He too removed his basketball shoes and sandwiched my dwarfed boots between his pair and his brother's. He then ducked into the tent, taking a spot next to the Captain. As a first-year Dukie, the Freshman had, of course, never tented before. His enthusiasm for tenting, however, could hardly be equaled; he had undoubtedly heard his brother's stories of Krzyzewskiville. But often his desire to tent seemed to surpass even his fondness for basketball. He insisted on strict adherence to tenting policies and what he deemed the "integrity" of the line. While other tent members might hope to avoid a shift thanks to a grace period called during inclement weather, the Freshman would beg line monitors not to be so kind. A snowstorm might bring his tent to the verge of collapsing, and still he would continue tenting. Nevertheless, his presence as a member of our group was welcome: his devotion to being in Krzyzewskiville made it easy for us to convince him to take extra shifts.

I had the tent halfway zipped when a soft voice drifted in. "Hold on, I'm just taking off my shoes." I unzipped the flap and pulled it aside to reveal the next tent member to arrive—the Pre-Med Student, a biology major, whose shy voice belies her enthusiasm for basketball. We, her tent mates, are always astonished at her fervor during a game. With a painted face, half blue and half white, she can be heard screaming above the entire crowd. Her lack of inhibitions inside Cameron surprises those of us who know her well, since she is known to be too shy even to ask questions in class. Her reticence is rather a shame, because when she does speak her comments reveal a keen intelligence. But being in Cameron is different from what anyone might suppose, and better for a girl who, timid and alone, becomes part of a larger voice in which she can still hide.

Tonight, the Pre-Med Student's face was not decorated in

unevenly dried blue and white. Instead, shades of pink high-lighted her otherwise pale cheeks, no doubt painted by the cutting wind. Wearing many layers of clothing beneath a heavy wool coat, she spoke of the likelihood of falling ill. "Aaron!" she exclaimed when she saw me, "what are you doing without a jacket on? Don't you know how the cold can affect your immune system?" This concern must stem from her medical school preparations. I admit that the possibility of sickness was not remote; illness, however, becomes a minor sacrifice in order to see the fever pitch of a basketball game inside Cameron on a wintry night.

"I was just going to put my coat back on," I answered as she closed her pink umbrella, set it on the ground, and stepped inside the tent. She moved toward the spot on the other side of the Captain. The gray of sleepless nights had settled underneath her eyes, and the weight of her tattered backpack knocked me off balance when it grazed my shoulder as she passed. No doubt she had it packed with all the trappings of a student on the path to medical school. Yet, she is only a sophomore, and those books and their related workload could still inspire her to change her mind and choose another less demanding path.

The Pre-Med Student was not the only focused and driven student in Tent 25. With her came a fifth tent member, a religion major with ambitions of being a lawyer. However, aside from their mutual desire to attend grueling professional schools, the Pre-Med Student and the Pre-Law Student could not have been more different. An incessant talker, the third-year Pre-Law Student insisted on being heard. Her entrance was announced by ceaseless chatter that everyone tried desperately to defer. When she stepped inside the tent, complaining about the temperature, the Captain saved me the trouble of responding by interrupting her. "Shoes, please," he said, and pointed toward her feet. The Pre-Law Student rolled her eyes, as I had done minutes earlier at the same request, pushed into my hands her oversized designer handbag, and bent down to untie the laces of her tennis shoes. I stood next to her, holding her purse, while she wrestled her shoes off. It was as if our tent suddenly included the luxury of a doorman.

As I watched the Pre-Law Student, I couldn't help but notice how this girl had accessorized a matching purse and tennis shoes, no doubt chosen to accent the green of her sweatpants. I will deprive her here of further description, although I'm certain she would object, because no sooner than she had seated herself next to the Pre-Med Student than did three others appear outside the tent, removing their shoes and ready to claim a spot inside. The first to enter was the Engineer, followed by the Public Policy Major, both of whom were juniors, and not merely friends; in fact, truth be told, the Engineer was not cordially welcomed in the tent, but he was the boyfriend of the Public Policy Major, and to include her was to include him. He, in turn, then invited a friend from his fraternity — the third member of the entering trio, the Math Major. This gentleman was often more tolerable, responsible, and civil than was his fraternity brother. However, his relationships with his fellow tenters were occasionally strained: he did not always arrive for his tent shifts on time.

Perhaps in other settings some of these students would rarely spend a minute interacting. But in this city, and for their team, tenters tend to ignore their standard social division.

The Engineer and the Math Major did not arrive empty-handed. Each one carried a twelve-pack of what looked to be the cheapest beer they could find. The Captain's eyes focused on the beer, and the vein in his forehead became more pronounced. The two frat brothers took no notice; in fact, the Engineer may have spent more time deciding on the best place for his alcohol than he had spent on his outfit or, judging from the odor, his hygiene. If I remember correctly, he had worn the same flannel shirt and faded jeans yesterday. As for his frayed Duke hat, I doubt it ever comes off. I've often suspected it to be sewn to his scalp. His girlfriend, the Public Policy Major, waited as he took a seat, with his beer to his left. She sat down on his other side and pulled her long blonde hair back from her tanned face and into a ponytail.

As the Math Major set his drinks next to the Engineer's and took the seat between the alcohol and the Freshman, yet another K-villite strode in. He wore a black wool coat and carried under his arm not beer, as those before him had, but a play of Shakespeare's, the title of which I could not make out. He is an English major, and a dedicated one at that. Indeed, I remember often seeing him reading in the tent while huddled under numerous layers of clothes and blankets. He would leave a single hand out in the numbing cold to turn pages. This year marked his third year at Duke, but only his second season in K-ville. He had not chosen to tent during his freshman year; but having lost a year seemed to fuel his dedication to K-ville. His pride and pleasure in Duke basketball were perhaps the most persuasive of anyone belonging in the tent: I never once heard the English Major complain about any of the standard grievances regarding tenting policy or the frigid weather (despite winter's valiant attempts to evoke an objection). His lack of protests were in spite of his having spent the most time in line of all the members of our tent.

The English Major seated himself next to the Public Policy Major while I slid my arms into the sleeves of my coat and fastened its buttons. But before I could move to take my seat in the circle that was taking shape in the tent, the three final members arrived, shortly after nine. The first was an economics major, a sophomore and an avid fan. Her enthusiasm can be attributed in part to her parents, who themselves had graduated from Duke. As do many children of alumni, she had been planning to attend Duke since before entering high school. She claims that her reasons had nothing to do with basketball, but I find this statement difficult to believe. (She has shown me a picture of herself at a game, taken when she was three years old.)

The Economics Major settled in next to the Pre-Med Student as the Sociology Major strolled in. I had encountered this tenter only while switching shifts. I knew his major, and that he is a junior; otherwise, I can tell you very little. To the best of my knowledge, he has a proclivity for partying and sleeping.

He had in his hands a six-pack—perhaps he was worried that the Engineer and the Math Major were not planning to share. He took a seat next to the Economics Major and blocked the entrance to the tent while placing the drinks in his lap.

The final tenter to arrive at the entrance to the now crowded tent was a sophomore Women's Studies Major. Her usual attire of baggy jeans and a hooded sweatshirt had given way to sweatpants and a black ski jacket. I zipped closed the flap behind her, knowing that she, the twelfth person, would be the last to enter. She edged around the Sociology Major and moved into the circle between the Freshman and the Math Major. As she sat she chided them: "Can't you boys make room for a lady?"

Now you know the twelve who inhabit our tent, and I daresay you would be troubled to find a more diverse collection of students. Because most people's enthusiasm for tenting declines after freshman year, assembling a group of tenters becomes more of a challenge. When organizing the tent, you ask your friends to invite their friends, and with any luck, enough people are interested. But the resulting group can sometimes be a strange assortment of companions.

My eyes glided over the faces of my fellow tenters as I looked for a spot to sit in what had, minutes ago, been an empty tent. As I begrudgingly squeezed into the thin gap between the Pre-Law Student and the Economics Major, I asked, "Does anyone have suggestions for what to do tonight?"

"Let's start the drinking!" suggested the Engineer.

"It seems you already have," snapped the Pre-Law Student,

and everyone laughed, including the Engineer, who, I noticed, did not disagree.

The Captain asked, "Anyone want to go outside and throw a football around?" The Freshman showed interest, but no one else.

"I would," said the Math Major, "but in case you haven't noticed, it's raining."

The Captain shrugged, and the tent fell back into silence while we searched for ideas of how to pass the time.

The Pre-Med Student made a quiet suggestion. "Why don't we just try to get some work done?" she questioned. The tent once again erupted into laughter, but I doubt she had intended for her words to be a joke. Her cheeks, which had returned to their normal pale color once inside the tent, became pink again, and she lowered her eyes.

The laughter faded, and we turned again to watching each other think while listening to the steady rain above our heads. The people with alcohol opened their beers. The Captain stared at the drinkers but would say nothing unless one of them spilled the contents in his tent. Others began rummaging through bags to occupy themselves. The English Major cracked open his Shakespeare, and now I could read the title on the cover: *Othello*.

Since all twelve members of Tent 25 were seated inside, we were confused when the tent flap was unzipped from the outside. Into the tent came a soft, orange glow as well as the head of an unexpected visitor. Even in the muted light, we could see that the face of this intruder did not belong to a fellow tenter, or indeed to any student. What hair he had left was gray, and the skin on his cheeks and around his eyes had the wrinkles of too many winters.

"Excuse me, guys," said the stranger's baritone voice, "am I interrupting something? Do you mind if I come in and ask a couple of questions?"

"Seems you already have asked a couple of questions," the Sociology Major remarked as he squeezed against the Economics Major to allow room for the visitor to get out of the rain. The stranger showed no sign of having heard the sarcastic answer.

The flap opened wider and our visitor entered.

"You're welcome to have a seat," said the Captain, pointing to the space that had now opened between the Sociology and English Majors, "but first, could you take off your shoes? Otherwise, you might rip the floor of the tent."

"Certainly," replied the man, before slipping off his muddy sneakers and setting them outside, where the other shoes were growing soggy in the rain. Then he took his spot next to the Sociology Major while the English Major turned around to secure the tent flap. He rubbed his hands together for warmth and said, "It sure is cold out tonight."

Still not knowing who this gentleman was, or what he wanted, the English Major stopped tugging at the stuck zipper, unwrapped his gray wool scarf, and passed it to the stranger.

"Thanks," said the guest, and then he added, "My name's Rodney Hutchinson, and I'm a reporter with the *Times*." The curiosity in the tent dissipated with the revelation of the man's profession. K-villers expect to see reporters poking around the city, especially the night before the Carolina game. "I'm sorry to intrude like this," he continued in his oddly courtly manner, "But I couldn't help noticing all of the people walking into this tent."

"It's no intrusion at all," responded the Captain, "You're welcome to sit with us and ask any question you'd like. I'm sorry there's not more room in here, but in a tent designed for an intimate cast of twelve, an unlucky thirteenth doesn't fit too well." He chuckled at his own joke, as did the Freshman. Then he added, "I wish we could be a bit more interesting, but we've been sitting in silence for the past few minutes trying to decide on a way to entertain ourselves. The two nights of personal checks are generally pretty rowdy, since a quarter of the school comes out to K-ville. But the rain has put a damper on the atmosphere."

"Not much pleasure to be found out here," said the Engineer. "We've got no heat and no television. If I were you, I'd go inside where there's electricity and running water." Pressing the cold, metal rim of a can to his cracked lips, the Engineer tilted his head toward the sky and took a long draught of his beer, downing in three gulps what had to have been a nearly full container. He crushed the empty aluminum in his hand and threw it past the head of our friendly visitor and out of the tent.

"Not to worry!" proclaimed the reporter, disregarding the can that had grazed his ear while the English Major returned to pulling at the tent's zipper. "I've got some questions about K-ville that will provide a nice diversion. I'm a Duke alum, so my editor thought I might be the best person to send down to Durham to do a story on Krzyzewskiville before the big game with Carolina. Although I went to school here, things have changed a lot since I graduated back in '68. To be honest, I don't particularly care for the publicity that K-ville gets. We fans were just as enthusiastic and creative back when I was here, even though at that time the teams weren't always as good. But the media tries to pretend that Krzyzewskiville created the infamous atmosphere inside of Cameron. That's just not true. We didn't have anything like this for getting into games, but don't think we never spent the night outside waiting in line. As for our antics once the games began, half of those cheers you do were created years before the tenting tradition.

"But enough of my complaints—I just wanted to let all of you know where I stand on the phenomenon of K-ville. Now, if you would, please humor me if my questions seem a bit simple. K-ville doesn't make much sense to me, and I'm still trying to figure this whole tenting thing out."

"So are we," joked the Economics Major, and everyone laughed. But her comment was accurate.

The Math Major added, "I didn't put this much time into my college applications."

The laughter dissipated as the journalist persisted, saying, "I know this is a broad question, but can someone explain to me how this tenting process works?"

"Well," said The Captain with a haughty air in his voice, "since I'm not only the leader and captain of this tent but also its most senior and experienced member, I'm probably the best person to give you a basic idea of the system." Most of the other tenters returned to what they had been doing before the reporter's arrival: the drinkers went back to drinking, the English Major went back to reading, and so on. If you're a tenting veteran perusing this account of the evening's events, you may skip the next few lines if you so wish. As for anyone else, it might help you to hear the Captain's explanation, so I'll include it for you here.

"The problem is," started the Captain, "that every year the rules change, at least a little bit. Sometimes the number of games for which we tent is altered. Sometimes the games we tent for are changed — although we always tent for the contests against Carolina. And anything down to the number of people required to be in K-ville at a specific time can vary from year to year. Thus, what I tell you pertaining to this year might not have been true in years past, and it might be changed further in future seasons. The first thing you have to understand is that Krzyzewskiville is a city. Just like any city, it has its share of problems. We have issues to manage concerning crime, sanitation — even fire code regulations. For better or for worse, the governing of K-ville is left to the Duke Student Government, DSG. Each year, the president-elect of DSG chooses a new head line monitor. This person, in turn, becomes a cross between a sheriff and a mayor for K-ville."

"I'd say more of a dictator," scoffed the Women's Studies Major.

The Captain plowed on with his explanation. "The head line

monitor then chooses his line monitors for the coming basketball season. Recently, the head line monitors have been better about making the process seem more diplomatic by holding interviews for the lesser line monitor positions. But, to be honest, they still tend to choose their friends. Unless you know the right person, it can be hard to become a part of that clique."

"Wait a minute," interrupted the reporter, "why would someone want to be a line monitor? It seems like it would be more work both to tent and to patrol the tent village. Or are these line monitors the more dedicated fans?"

None of the other tenters overhearing the explanation could withhold our amusement at Rodney's naive question. "The more *dedicated* fans?" sneered the Engineer.

"Only if you measure dedication by social connections!" exclaimed the Math Major.

"I was just about to get to that," snapped the Captain, trying to quell our laughter. "One of the perks to being a line monitor is that you don't have to tent."

A look of comprehension came to Rodney's face. "Oh, I see," he said as he made hasty scribbles on a small notebook he had pulled from his pocket. "Now it makes sense. So the line monitors are guaranteed seats — they use the position as a way to get in. So what's involved in being a line monitor?"

"Nothing," chuckled the Pre-Law Student, before the Captain continued his explanation.

"Well," he said, glancing sidelong at the girl who had interrupted him, "that's not entirely true. Being head line monitor is nearly a full time job during the basketball season, requiring twenty to thirty hours of work per week in order to coordinate the events, public relations, and scheduling of K-ville. As for the other line monitors, they don't have to do as much as a tenter. Their main job is to run tent checks and screen people as they enter the games. For this, they have a section of the first two rows on the TV side reserved for them. Perhaps it's a bit unfair to the tenters, but it's not a bad system."

"TV side?" questioned the reporter.

The Pre-Med student looked up from a binder of notes to answer, "That's the side of the arena seen during the games as the television cameras pan across the court to follow the action."

"Ah, I see," said the journalist as he continued jotting down notes. "Okay, I think I understand how K-ville is governed, so to speak. But how does the line work? What did you mean by 'tent checks'?"

"Well," resumed the Captain, "the basic idea is that each tent receives a number, and that tent number then represents a group of up to twelve people. Someone from a given tent has to be in K-ville twenty-four hours a day, seven days a week, unless a grace period is called. A grace of at least thirty minutes is always called immediately after a tent check, for example, and a grace can be called during a televised away game, a woman's basketball game, inclement weather, and so on. Of course, if you mandate that someone from each tent has to be in K-ville at all times, then you have to devise a way of checking for constant tent occupancy, right? Hence, the line monitors hold tent checks.

By way of an annoying bullhorn siren, line monitors will notify the K-villers of a check. This check could be at two in the afternoon, at two in the morning, or anytime between. If a member of your tent is not present when the line monitors call your tent number, it counts as a missed check. Two missed tent checks, and your tent gets bumped to the back of the tenting line."

"How far is the back of the line?"

"Well, it varies. During the early tenting period, called 'blue tenting,' the line can't reach more than fifty tents. But blue tenting has stricter rules. At night, a tent has to have eight members in K-ville for a check instead of just one, meaning that blue tenting is reserved for the more 'hard-core' fans. Blue tenters can begin tenting at any time. The earliest blue tent this year was set up the day after Christmas." Rodney smiled as he scribbled down a note.

" 'White tenting' is the later tenting period," explained The Captain. "It generally starts between two weeks and ten days before a game. At this time, the rules change: one person must be present for tent checks at all times, up until two nights before the game, when personal checks start. That's what we're in now—personal checks. During white tenting there are generally around a hundred tents—that's about twelve hundred students, or roughly two-thirds of the student section inside the stadium. You don't want to get bumped to the back of that line.

"As for personal checks, everyone in a tent has to be accounted for at three of the five personal checks that will be called sometime during the two nights before a game. Once you've finished that, it's on to the main event in Cameron."

The reporter took a few more notes in silence. It seemed that the Captain had completed his explanation. When Rodney finished writing, he looked up and asked, "So what do you guys do out here in the tents?"

"Some people like to get work done," murmured the Pre-Med Student.

"Some people like to get drunk," added the Women's Studies Major, gesturing toward the Engineer, who, by this point, was opening his third beer.

"Well, how about tonight?" questioned the reporter. "What are you guys planning to do now?"

"That's what we were trying to decide before you came along," said the Public Policy Major while looking for a dry spot to place her purse. "Normally, personal checks are like one giant party, since all the tenters have gathered in K-ville. But with the rain, there's not much to do tonight."

The reporter scribbled a few more notes on his pad before setting it aside. By this time, everyone in the group had returned his attention to the discussion. Rodney looked around at the collection of students gathered inside the crowded tent. He thought for a few moments, then said, "I know a way to make the most of your idle time here."

This statement aroused the interest of all the tenters, but it was the Women's Studies Major who asked, "What do you suggest?"

"Well," began the reporter, "There are twelve of you here, and there's plenty of time to spend—so, why don't each of you recite a story that pertains in some way to Duke basketball and Krzyzewskiville? We can make it a contest, and even offer a prize. Perhaps the winner saves him- or herself a tent shift for another game."

A soft murmur followed the journalist's suggestion. Soon, the Pre-Law Student asked the inevitable. "That sounds like a great idea," she said, "but how would we choose the winner?"

"I'm glad you asked that," Rodney responded, "and if none of you mind, I will stay out here for a while, and play Host and judge of this little contest. Being a Duke alum, I love Duke basketball, and I'm out here to get the story of K-ville. I have nothing to gain in victory or defeat, so at least I'll be impartial. I also want to hear what stories you know about the history of this tradition you value so highly. This should be an interesting experience. Yes, let us tell some Krzyzewskiville Tales!"

And so it was decided. We would pass the time until the final personal check relating stories we had heard about K-ville or tales from our personal experiences. This reporter would serve as the Host of our game, and with any luck we could teach him about the history of our tent city and convince him of its worthiness as well.

I will now try to recreate the stories told this evening as authentically as my memory will allow, but keep in mind that the majority of these words are not my own. You are privy to these tales, listening, as I did, to an otherwise unwritten history of

K-ville. Whatever was said I do not necessarily endorse, but have provided here for you to read. I intend to give the stories of fellow tenters a public voice. Please know, I cannot control the mouths of others, nor would I report in purposeful error their stories. As the recorder of these accounts, I feel obliged to provide you all of the tales, including whatever fallacies or slanderous words were spoken. Thus, if you experienced a specific event in K-ville, and my recounting of it is not identical to your memory, I cannot be held responsible for the words of other people. Also, if in some way I defame a person, an administration, or even another school (such as Carolina), I have not done so with malicious intent. I am a mere servant of factual events. Please, keep this in mind as I continue the tales, but feel free to set them aside if your expectations are failed.

"Because we need a fair way to decide who goes first," continued the Host, "we will draw straws." A few moments of chatter passed, all in agreement of the ordering process.

"Where are you going to find straws out here?" the Women's Studies Major asked.

"Not a problem," said the Host, and he unzipped a corner of the tent's flap, reached outside and unearthed a wet patch of grass. With his hand full of damp green blades, the Host turned his attention toward the tent's Captain and said, "Given your position, why don't you draw first?" And so he did, followed by his younger brother, then the Math Major, and so on and so forth until all of us held a blade of grass in our hands. As luck would have it, the task of telling the first story went to the Captain, who held the shortest straw. The rest of us breathed a sigh of relief; I doubt any of the other tenters could have recalled a story about K-ville as easily as the one whom fate had chosen to tell his anecdote first.

The Host turned to the Captain and joked, "It looks like your duties as leader have expanded. Since you hold the shortest blade of grass, you must begin your story and help your fellow tenters pass the time until their last personal check."

While taking a deep breath, the experienced senior searched his thoughts. I doubt a minute had passed before a story came to him and he said, "I know what tale to tell." He looked around at each of the other members in his tent to be certain of their attention. "Since it seems I've been chosen to start, I should begin in a logical place. I can think of no better way to lay the foundation for our evening's revelations about K-ville than to tell the story of how this tent city first sprung from the ground. Now, with your attention, and perhaps the blessing of Coach K himself, I'll give you the story of how Krzyzewskiville began."

THE CAPTAIN

The First Part Follows

nce upon a time, before the days of tenting, when Duke had yet to win a national basketball championship and the school's athletic reputation conjured up images of football dominance, its students were setting standards for cheering excellence. Before the television camera appeared in college arenas, before ESPN sold the country NCAA basketball, the students of Duke University transformed taunting into an art form. In fact, Duke students were wildly enthusiastic basketball fans even before their beloved arena took the name of the famed Duke coach and athletics director Edmund Cameron and they earned their moniker, the Cameron Crazies. Today Duke basketball fans have become sporting legend, and the evolution of the Crazies has become myth. Some people like to date Krzyzewskiville back to 1986, but its foundations were laid nearly a half-century prior.

A man by the name of Bradley R. Walton — Brad, to his friends — ranks as one of Duke's first diehard fans. Born in 1924 and raised in the southern part of Durham County, Brad came of age amid the Duke-UNC rivalry: his uncle's small horse farm, where he lived, was halfway between the two institutions.

Growing up on the farm, Brad lived with his aunt and uncle and their son Sam, his cousin. The two cousins had been born only a month apart, and because Brad was sent to live in Durham at the age of five, they were raised as brothers. They shared a room, worked the farm together, and attended the same school. Sam and Brad were inseparable and the best of friends, but, as would any pair of friends or brothers, they did occasionally disagree. Most notably they clashed over the Duke-UNC rivalry.

The year was 1940, and basketball was still a young sport in North Carolina. But the semiannual games between the neighboring schools along Tobacco Road carried an intensity not unlike that of today's rivalry: both programs were laying the groundwork for a rise to national prominence. The new decade saw the first meeting between the two schools in a brand-new basketball facility on Duke's recently built West Campus, Duke Indoor Stadium. As legend has it, the first design of the building was sketched on the back of a matchbook by Edmund Cameron and another familiar personality in Duke athletics — the man for whom the football stadium is named, Wallace Wade.

On a mid-January evening, Brad sat at the dinner table with his aunt, uncle, and cousin, having just finished a piece of apple pie baked in celebration of his sixteenth birthday. Brad stood and began stacking the dirty plates to take to the sink when his uncle said, "Just hold on a minute. We're not done here yet. First you need to open your present." His uncle handed him a thin envelope with Brad's name scrawled on front.

"Thanks, Uncle Danny," said Brad as he took the envelope. He pulled his chair closer to the table and slipped his finger under the sealed flap. Brad pinched the two thin pieces of paper inside the envelope between his thumb and finger and pulled them out. He read the words aloud, "February 23, 1940, Duke vs. UNC–Chapel Hill, Duke Indoor Stadium." Brad stared at the tickets as a smile spread across his face. He looked up and said, "Tickets to the Duke-UNC game! I can't believe it. How'd you get these?"

"What, you think your old uncle doesn't have any connections?"

"No . . . I didn't mean it like that. I just . . . just can't believe it. Thanks!"

"Happy birthday," said Brad's aunt. "Now you two boys enjoy those."

"Who said I was going to bring Sam?" joked Brad.

"That's fine. Why would I want to go see Duke play anyway?" answered Sam as he reached over and snatched the tickets. Brad sprang from his chair and darted toward Sam, who, in turn, sprinted around to the other side of the table. The two boys raced around the house laughing and hurling insults about each other's favorite school.

"Snobs!" cried Sam, in reference to Duke students.

"Hicks!" retorted Brad, describing Chapel Hill kids.

These insults continued for the next month until the day of the game. At that game in 1940, and probably at every game to this day, the stadium was packed with fans anticipating the contest between the neighboring schools just eight miles apart. Brad and Sam entered the new 8,000-seat arena—which would give way to the 9,314-person setup of today—built just west of the main section of the men's campus. (In 1940 all women students would have lived on East Campus, the former women's college, which eventually would become an all-freshman campus.) At the time, Duke Indoor Stadium was the largest enclosed arena in the South, although it is difficult to imagine such a distinction for Cameron today. It was often described as a "cheap knockoff" of the Palestra, the stadium in Philadelphia on which it was roughly modeled.

When Brad and Sam entered the arena, their eyes widened at the sight of 8,000 spectators—more people than they had ever seen gathered in one building—all anticipating the clash between the Blue Devils of Duke University and the White Phantoms of the University of North Carolina, as they were known in the days before they were the Tar Heels.

Bradley and Sam found their seats. They were in the last row on the side where the broadcasting booth now hangs. The two cousins sat down and hardly spoke as their eyes darted around the stadium. They saw an arena scarcely unlike what it is today, at least in terms of general setup: the same iron beams arched over the hardwood and formed a crest at the peak of the roof;

28

white bucket seats lined the upper dignitary areas; and, on the floor below, wooden bleachers surrounded the court. Filling every spot on those bleachers were, of course, Duke students. Even at the stadium's inception, the best seats in the house were reserved for Duke undergraduates. Standing to cheer during games had yet to become protocol, however, and all the men wore coats and ties and women wore their best Sunday dresses —very unlike today's blue- and white-painted screaming fans.

One aspect of Cameron missing at the building's completion, one which we today take for granted, was air-conditioning. Even in February, a building containing 8,000 enthusiastic fans could still become hot and steamy. Cameron, however, was not air-conditioned until the 2001–2002 season, more than sixty years after it had begun playing host to hundreds of athletic events, ceremonies, speeches, and concerts.

Brad turned to his cousin, who had his arms crossed over his chest trying to hide his dirt-stained and age-worn overalls. Indeed, the two, similarly clad, looked out of place among the well-dressed crowd, but Brad took no notice of the distinction. He whispered to his cousin, "This is the most amazing place I've ever seen."

Samuel had just the opposite reaction to the majesty of Duke's new arena. "It's too big," he griped, "we're never going to be able to see anything from up here! Why did they have to make this place so big? It's not like this many people will always want to come see a Duke game. These people are only here because they're playing UNC. This place is just a waste of space. At least tickets will probably be easy to get."

"Are you kidding, Sam, this place is incredible!" responded Brad.

"Well," began Sam, "I hope I never live to see the day that UNC builds a huge, gaudy stadium that they'll almost never be able to fill."

And so the two boys countered back and forth for the rest of the game. Sam cheered in the loudest voice he could muster every time UNC made a basket or Duke missed. Not to be outdone, Brad lost his voice screaming for Duke throughout the game. In the end, no amount of cheering from Brad or anyone else would help the Blue Devils: Carolina defeated the home team with a score of 31–27.

On the walk back to the farm, Sam taunted Brad so ruthlessly that an onlooker might have thought Sam had won the game himself. Yet Sam's jeers did little more than cultivate Brad's desire to one day attend Duke and become one of the students who lived for the basketball team.

I regret to have to end this first part of my story on a sad note: Bradley Walton never made it to the student section of Cameron. Even as he and his cousin watched the basketball game in February of 1940, a ruthless dictator was ravaging Europe. Before they were ever college students, Brad and Sam found themselves in the northern deserts of Africa fighting a "fox" in the service of a murderer. And it is there that I shall leave the tale of these two gentlemen for now.

Daniel had been a Duke fan his entire life; it was a passion he had never questioned. Duke factored perhaps larger than religion in his upbringing. He had been raised with constant reminders from his father about how he would someday attend Duke. "If you work hard enough in school," his father would say, "one day you'll go to Duke University and be a Blue Devil. You'll get to sit with the students in Cameron." His dad also jokingly admonished him, "If you do poorly in school, you'll wind up at Carolina."

Inspired by the incentive to work hard in school (not to mention a damn good reason not to slack off), Daniel found himself bound for his freshman year at Duke. Most of all he anticipated the basketball games his father had spoken of so often, because despite his family's fanaticism for the school and its basketball program, Daniel had yet to see a game in person. That changed soon after he arrived on campus: he attended every game played in Cameron during his four years at Duke, from the first tip of the season opener in the fall of his freshman year to the final second of the season's last game in the spring of his senior year. By far the best of these match-ups involved one of the most impressive offensive performances by a single player in the history of Duke basketball, during a game that has been called one of the greatest in the Duke-UNC rivalry.

The game on February 23, 1963, ended in one of fourteen Atlantic Coast Conference wins for the Duke program that year, giving the team a flawless league record that helped it along to the Final Four. The star of that game was Art Heyman, the first Duke player to go number one overall in the NBA draft. The All-American scored a career-high 40 points, 24 of which came in the final period, to lead the team to a 106–93 defeat of Carolina. With twenty-two seconds remaining in the game, Heyman left his home court for the last time to a three-minute standing ovation from the Duke Blue Bedlamites — the name given the student-section fans before they became the Cameron Crazies.

Heyman's performance was certainly a memory to cherish, as was the win. But more important, in those three minutes of applause, Daniel came to truly understand his father's love of Duke basketball. After the game, he went back to his room and wrote a letter to his father. The letter said

Dear Dad,

By the time you read this letter, you will undoubtedly know the result of Duke's most recent basketball victory over Carolina. You will have read the news reports and will know how the game progressed. You'll also have read about the unbelievable offensive performance of Art Heyman. But I wanted to send you my own thoughts on the game, something you won't find in any newspapers. I want to tell you that I finally understand why you taught me to love Duke basketball.

Today's victory was not merely a defeat of an arch rival, nor was it simply another victory toward a perfect conference record. Today, Duke basketball was about the Duke student community. When Heyman left the court to applause that shook the floors and walls of the stadium, I saw in every face the spirit of this school. It was the students, the faculty, the alumni, and even the unaffiliated fans joining together to support a Duke victory. Basketball may be the most prominent example of such support, but never has a day gone by when I haven't received the same in a classroom. The Duke community will appreciate any accomplishment, that's for sure. But more important, and perhaps proved more so by other experiences that didn't produce stars and victory, the Duke community will always be here to support its students in their more trying hours, be they in academic struggle, personal tragedy, or any other challenge.

Duke basketball is an extension of the Duke spirit. The players are students, just like us. They are our colleagues, our peers and, above all, our friends. We celebrate their victories and taste the same bitterness of defeat because together we are a student body. We are a community. Now I know why you love this school. Now I know why you sent me here. I can never thank you enough for the opportunity you have given me, and I can only hope to have the chance to pass this experience on to my children as well.

Always with thanks and love,

Daniel

James entered an already crowded commons room on a cold evening in late February of 1986. It was a Thursday night, and just as there had been every other Thursday night, a game of Quarters was taking place in the selective-living group of Mirecourt. This is not the time or place to explain the intricacies of that particular drinking game, although some here may know it very well.

But I digress: let us return to that February night in 1986.

The highly anticipated UNC game was fast approaching, to be played on Sunday, March 2. As is usually the case around campus in the few days before the Carolina game, the discussion in Mirecourt eventually turned to basketball. James had a particular interest in this match-up, not only because of the opponent but also because of some of the fans who would attend. James's father, Daniel Walton, would be at the game; so too would his grandfather, Bradley Walton. In honor of his father's sixty-second birthday, Daniel had procured three tickets for himself, his father, and a friend of his father's. Because two earlier generations of Walton Duke basketball fans would also be at the game, James wanted to be certain that he would be visible among the students. Concerned with how to secure one of the best seats in the house, he initiated a discussion about how early he and his friends should begin to line up for the game.

"When do we want to get in line?" asked James.

"The game is on Sunday, right?" said one of James's friends. "I'll bet people start getting out there Saturday morning."

"I suppose we can get out there around then," said another friend. "Maybe mid-morning or early afternoon. When do you think we should get out there?"

"I don't know," answered James, "but I need to get good seats. My dad and grandfather will be there. I want them to be able to see me from the stands."

A few more rounds of Quarters (and plenty of drinks) later, someone said, "Hey, why don't we just go out there tonight? That way we're sure to beat everyone in line."

"If we get out there now," said another person, "we'll have to sleep outside for three days. I'm not doing that."

James thought about how to form the line that very night without freezing. "I have an idea," he said at last. "Why don't we just pitch some tents?"

Perhaps under normal—and sober—circumstances, the notion of being outside for three straight days in the cold of February simply for good seats for a two-hour basketball game would have seemed foolish. But since this idea would assure the group a prime location in Cameron for the Carolina game, they decided to give it a try and set up four tents.

Word of tents being pitched on the grass in front of Cameron began to spread on campus that day. Discovering that people were already waiting outside Cameron for the UNC game, other students rushed to stake their places in line. And posted on a pole fixed in the front of this makeshift campground was a piece of cardboard—the back of an old pizza box, from what I hear—

and on it was written the word *Krzyzewskiville*. I guess the name stuck.

Now we have to remember that the Krzyzewskiville of today is not at all like it was in the early years. Although line monitors existed, they didn't wield the same powers they hold now, nor were they out policing the integrity of the line days in advance to ensure that no one wrongfully jumped ahead of an established group. There weren't any rules governing the tenters; there were no tent shifts. K-ville was a free-for-all, and if you wanted your place in line, you had to stay out there and protect it yourself. But that first group of kids, and all of the tenters that followed them that year, made it abundantly clear: they had been outside in line for days, and nobody was going to get in front of them. A second sign appeared in what quickly came to be known as K-ville:

DON'T EVEN THINK ABOUT
CUTTING THIS LINE . . .
WE'VE BEEN HERE SINCE
THURSDAY——
WE'LL *KILL* YOU!

So that was how K-ville began. As you can see, it wasn't created by the administration to show school spirit, and it wasn't a prefabricated city with the current long list of rules and requirements. Krzyzewskiville is the offspring of spontaneity, and Duke's most devoted fans flock to it with one purpose: to earn the best seats possible in Cameron Indoor Stadium.

As for James, he got his reward. He was in the front row at

center court for the game. And all he had to do was look up across the stadium to see his father, Daniel, and his grandfather, Brad. In a game between two of the best teams in the country, the Blue Devils edged out the Tar Heels, 82–74. Duke was en route to a first-place finish in the ACC, a Final Four appearance, and a final record of 37–3 — the winningest season in the history of collegiate basketball to that date.

Forty-six years after his first experience in Cameron, Bradley Walton sat in the same stadium he'd visited in his youth, looking upon two generations of Duke fans that his love for the school had helped create. He finally saw Duke triumph over Carolina in person. But the victory was truly bittersweet. This time his best friend was not in the seat next to him to share the experience. Although he had another ticket and could have invited someone to attend the game with him and his son, Brad chose to leave a seat empty in memory of his cousin, Samuel, who had not come home from the fighting in the north of Africa.

THE ENGINEER

When the Captain had finished his story, there was hardly anyone who would not agree that it was a noble tale, well worth remembering for the sake of Krzyzewskiville and the people who helped to create it. Our Host laughed and proclaimed, "That certainly was a good start. I had read that K-ville began in 1986, but as I mentioned earlier, even I had spent nights outside before the UNC games. Granted, Coach K wasn't around when I was here, but we certainly had our own form of Krzyzewskiville."

"I've heard alumni complain," answered our Captain, "because they think we date sleeping out for games to 1986. But if that's your response, than you have not listened to my story. We date Krzyzewskiville to 1986 — not tenting. I don't want to hear another person complain about tenting having started before K-ville. We know that the Crazies existed before 1986, and we've never claimed otherwise."

"That's true. And students even tent at other schools," remarked the English Major, stroking his goatee. "I have friends at Wake Forest and Georgia Tech who tell me about spending the night in line for their home games against Duke. But sleeping outside is not what makes Krzyzewskiville special. Nor would other fans' tenting experiences be the same in a tent village of a different name. Perhaps the other stories you'll hear will convince you that the uniqueness of K-ville stems from the inimitable Duke student body."

The Host nodded in response to the English Major's comments and glanced at the Captain as though he wanted to argue with him about the origins of the tenting tradition at Duke. Instead, he scribbled a few words in his spiral notebook, turned the page, and said, "We'd best get on with our competition. I'm curious to hear more about the developments in tenting since I graduated. Now, it's time to see who tells his story next. I suppose we could go in order of seniority. Tell me, are there any other seniors in the tent?" The Math Major motioned for the eye of the Host, who said, "Well, since you appear to be the only other senior, you will speak next—so long as you have a story to match our Captain's in historical value and entertainment."

The Engineer, who was so drunk that he had turned pale, could hardly sit straight. His head would fall onto his girlfriend's shoulder for a few seconds before he would jerk upright, only to slump over again moments later. Whenever he spoke he lowered his hat further over his eyes, and he refused to show any other member of the party the slightest courtesy. In an obnoxious, drunken voice he shouted and swore, "By the ceiling, halls, and court of Cameron, I know a story to match the Captain's!"

Our Host, seeing that the Engineer was drunk, said, "We've

chosen to order our tales by seniority, so let's follow that decision. Besides, we ought to let some more sober man tell us a story first. Let us hear what this other senior tenter would like to tell us."

"Oh, no," said the Engineer, "I sure as hell won't. I'll say what I want to say or else I'm out of here." Using his girlfriend's shoulder as a crutch, the Engineer made an attempt to stand. He had his right foot flat on the ground, and most of his weight balanced on his left knee. But when his hand slipped off his girlfriend's shoulder, he fell onto his back, his head in his girlfriend's lap. This tumble would not deter him, however; still on his back, he continued insisting that we should hear his story.

Seeing that the Engineer would not be quieted and no longer had the capacity to leave the tent, our Host retorted, "Fine then, tell away—but you're a damn fool. Alcohol has obviously gotten the better of you."

"Now listen up," said the Engineer, still talking to the heavens, "everyone! First of all, let me say that I am drunk. I can tell from the slur in my words and by the funny snorting noise coming from my nose. So if I say something offensive, blame it on the beer of Milwaukee, that's all I ask. Now, I shall tell you the story of a student in the Trinity School of Arts and Sciences and his girlfriend, and how a Pratt Engineering student made a fool of the Trinity kid."

The Sociology Major, who was nursing a third bottle of his own brew, spoke up and said, "Oh, shut up! Stop your damn, drunken BS. Besides, it will only make you look worse to speak ill of another person, and especially so if you bring his girlfriend into it. I'm sure you can find something else to talk about."

The drunken Engineer immediately responded, "Come on, Craig, I'm not saying that all girls are unfaithful, and I'm not saying that your girlfriend is cheating on you. Lord knows there are some good women out there. Why are you already angry at my story? I have a girlfriend, damn it, just like you do, but I'm not going to worry about her integrity. The way I see it, as long as she's making me happy," the Engineer paused, turned his head to survey the group, and flashed a wicked smile, "and I think you know what I mean, then it's not my place to be asking questions about the rest of her business."

Need I say anything more than that this Engineer wouldn't listen to reason and told his vulgar story just as he wanted? I regret to tell it here; thus I ask every well-raised person to please not think that I have any bad intentions. Remember that I am required, in good conscience, to recount all of the tales, or else falsify my material. Therefore, whoever does not want to read the Engineer's tale can feel free to turn to another tale, because he will discover plenty of stories, long and short, that cover history and dedication and Craziness of all sorts. The Engineer is a lowly person, and I have cautioned you of his shortcomings. So, keep that in mind and don't blame me for the words that follow. And besides, remember that this competition is just a game, and like all games, it should not be taken too seriously.

Once there was a Trinity student who was majoring in sociology, if my memory still serves me. As we all know quite well, the ease of this major is at the heart of numerous jokes on this campus. It gives the student many more hours of free time when compared to a person with a real major, such as myself. This sociology major's extra time allowed him to take additional shifts in the tent. He often picked up the slack for other members that took real classes and had to spend time both on homework and in labs. But he was, nevertheless, an extremely good-natured fellow. Apart from his choice of majors, I can hardly say a bad word. Despite his coming from a wealthy family, he always acted kindly. He was not one to flaunt his parents' money. And yet, his clothing was expensive, as were his other material tastes. The tent he pitched was filled with lavish goods—a couch, two air mattresses, and battery-powered lamps. He even left an extra laptop in his tent for his tent mates to use when he wasn't around. The boy I speak of was named Thomas R. Langland III, but those who knew him well simply called him Tom.

Tom was the founding member of Tent 5 in a K-ville of several years ago. He pitched his tent in late December, and through the first two weeks he slept in it alone every night. Of course there were eleven others belonging to his tent. They would all arrive later, once the semester began. None, however, was more important to him than his beautiful girlfriend, Lauren. Now, to describe Tom as ugly might be an exaggeration. Mind you, I'm no judge of the looks of men, but still, he had no business dating a girl as gorgeous as Lauren. The tangled brown curls covering his head seemed all the more unkempt when he stood next to Lauren, whose cascade of golden blonde hair framed an angelic face. The crystalline blue of her lively eyes would draw any man's gaze. Below her virtuous face was a long neck, lengthened more by her upturned chin. To say that this girl was simply beautiful would do little justice to her beguiling form. With this description in mind, her relationship with the cherubic Tom might seem somewhat suspect; it's my guess that his family's money played a part in her interest in him, for it certainly wasn't his academic prowess.

Tom, however, was in love. As any man so stricken, not to mention financially so at ease, he showered Lauren with lavish gifts. She responded in turn with little kisses on his plump cheeks. But that modest gesture was the extent of her physical affection, at least toward Tom. Lauren flaunted her purity. However, most who knew her personally (and many who knew her only by reputation) knew this purity to be a charade. Truth be told, this girl was no angel. Her past included multitudes of boyfriends and many more suitors. Lauren's penchant for flirting encouraged every boy she met to indulge in romantic fantasies about her.

One of these dreamers worked himself into the tent by befriending Tom. However, all he wanted was to be nearer to Lauren. His name was Charles and he was not the manliest of fellows. He was tall, lanky, and had a voice as high as a bird's.

Charles made it a point to stop by the tent frequently with the hope of finding Lauren within. In addition, he volunteered to spend nearly every night of the eight-person blue-tenting period jammed inside the well-furnished but crowded tent, hopeful that Lauren would be sleeping nearby—although she was never around without Tom in sight.

The date for the Carolina game was fast approaching. White tenting soon passed, and with ten days until the game, the blue-tenting period began. It was at this time that one of Tent 5's other nine members missed a check. He erroneously thought the siren could be heard from his room and decided to wait inside where it was warmer. This decision nearly cost Tent 5 its hard-earned place in line. Upon receiving the news of a missed check, Tom fell into such a rage that he immediately booted the culprit from the tent. Tom reasoned that the group couldn't afford the dreaded second miss that would send Tent 5 to the back of the hundred-tent line, and he no longer felt that his group could rely on this careless tenter.

Now that the occupancy of Tent 5 had unexpectedly shrunk to eleven, Thomas knew he would need to find someone to fill the final spot. Without a twelfth person, the group would be overextended, and the anxiety created during the tenting period would only be heightened. To find this additional person, Tom turned to an engineering friend who tutored him to offset his troubles with a core-curriculum math course. Steven was his name; he was quite an intelligent person, and dare I say handsome. School work caused him little concern, and his charm with the ladies turned his name into legend. Having met Thomas's gorgeous girlfriend, Steven was more than eager to join the tent. I imagine his having to tent for less than ten days to be a member of the fifth tent also helped his decision. I won't chance a guess as to which he thought more important: was it Lauren or the game against Carolina?

Finding Lauren alone in the tent seemed almost impossible, given her and Tom's near-constant companionship. Even when it was Lauren's shift, Tom would keep her company. This intrusion left little time for either Steven or Charles to privately approach Lauren; instead, each suitor devised a plan by which he could keep Tom separated from Lauren while in K-ville. You may ask, "Why in K-ville?" Let us not forget that these events unfolded on a college campus, a close-knit community where secrecy is perhaps more important than discretion. For the benefit of both Lauren's relationship and her reputation, the two courtiers knew their best chance for the fulfillment of their fantasies lay only in the secretive recesses of the tents of K-ville.

Steven's plan began quite simply. One afternoon Lauren came to relieve him at three o'clock, and while she arranged her sleeping bags in the tent, Steve seized the rare opportunity of finding the girl alone. He crept behind her, put his hand on her shoulder, and whispered in her ear, "You know, there are better ways to keep warm in the tent."

Not turning from her task but immediately understanding what Steven implied, Lauren gave a quick reply: "And I suppose you would be willing to show me if I asked."

"Of course I would," said Steven. He encircled her slender waist with his muscular arms. He then touched his lips to her cold ear and whispered, "I can even do so right now if you'll give me a chance."

Lauren leaned back into Steven. She let her blonde hair fall across his shoulders. But she stopped the advance of her suitor by saying, "Not today, Tom will be here any second. But I'll make a deal with you. If you can keep him away during one of my shifts, then you can be the man here instead of him."

Steven kissed her ear, then said, "Same time as today, this coming Wednesday. Tell Tom you can't make your shift, and ask him to cover it. If you can do that, I'll take care of the rest." As he was finishing his sentence, the tent flaps began to rustle, warning them that someone was about to enter. The two quickly broke their embrace a mere moment before Tom appeared at the entrance of Tent 5, untying his shoelaces.

After a casual greeting to his friend, Steven moved toward the door of the tent. As he passed by Tom he reminded him, "Tuesday at seven, don't forget our tutoring session."

Tuesday night came, the tutoring session began, and Steven could only hope that Lauren had followed his suggestion. It took the better part of an evening for Tom to understand what seemed to Steven like simple math. But what would you expect from someone who doesn't take real classes? When the two began the walk back to their rooms from the library, Steven started to lay the trap he had been rehearsing again and again in his mind. "Oh, by the way," he said, with exaggerated excitement, "I found a time when we don't have to worry about line checks. See, one of my friends is a line monitor, and he had an availability chart on his desk for all the line monitors. When he left the room for a minute I checked it out and noticed that they're all busy on Wednesdays from three to seven, which means they can't do a check then, so nobody has to be in the tent."

"Really?" asked Tom. "That would be great. I have to cover Lauren's shift tomorrow from three to five because she's got some review session, and then my shift is from five to seven."

Of course, Steven already knew these details, but, feigning ignorance, he responded, "Well, great, then you won't have to show up at all."

"I guess not. But are you absolutely sure? We can't risk another missed check."

"Of course I'm sure," Steven answered. "Besides, I can hear a tent check siren from my room, and since I'll be there studying all night there's absolutely no way we could miss one."

After Steven's numerous assurances, Tom felt comfortable skipping his shifts. Steve's meeting with Lauren could go as planned with no need to worry about an unwanted guest.

Let us not forget about Charles, however, whose infatuation with Lauren far surpassed that of Steven's. Being a romantic, and of the hopeless sort, it was not simply Charles's intention of sleeping with Lauren (although I imagine that the thought was in his mind as well). In addition to companionship, the young man sought love, which of course any wise man knows is a word of trickery, contrived by women in order to torment the world of men. But, I digress, and that is a story for another day. Now, let us return to Charles's plot and the way in which he sought to get Lauren alone in the tent.

That same Tuesday evening, Charles kept watch to see when Tom returned to his room. Charles lived next door to Tom, so he was able to wait for his arrival without looking too suspicious. Not as practiced in deceit as Steven, Charles struggled to devise a reason important enough to pull Tom away from his constant watch over Lauren. Mustering all the confidence a boy can when he's in love with the girlfriend of a good friend, Charles knocked on Tom's door, and when it opened he began with a bit of a mumble, "Tom, I was wondering if you could perhaps do me a favor. I've got an important package on the way, and someone needs to be around to make sure it arrives safely. I have a meeting which I can't cancel. It should be here between three and five tomorrow afternoon. Will you be around to watch for it and take it inside?"

Tom indifferently replied, "No problem, I'll make sure to be around for it."

"R—really?" stuttered Charles, surprised by the ease of the deception.

"Yeah, I have nothing else that I have to do. Besides, what are friends for?"

"Yeah . . . thanks." And Charles hurried back to his room, closing and locking the door. He hoped that Tom wouldn't remember Lauren's tent shift. Of course, he didn't realize what we already know: that Steven had been laying his own plans to meet with Lauren alone in the tent, which was precisely why Thomas could wait around the room for Charles's package. Charles, glowing in the triumph of his presumed victory, began to plan out what he hoped would happen the next day in Tent 5.

Wednesday found Steven beginning his tenting shift at one o'clock, and as is always the case when anticipation is high, time crept by. He lay on his back in the tent, covering himself with layers of sleeping bags, and he stared at the green and white pattern of the canvas ceiling. The hour rang two, and eventually three, and a few minutes thereafter, without a sound to foretell of her approach, Lauren entered. Steven sprang to his feet. He stared at the radiant red lips forming a mischievous smile. A moment of hesitation passed over the two students, and then they rushed into each other's arms. Lauren was the long coveted trophy Steven had sought for bragging rights. Steven was the man to satisfy Lauren while she pretended to love a boyfriend who had the wealth to provide her with lavish gifts. The details of their encounter I will leave to your vivid imaginations. I can, however, assure you that Steven kept his word about showing Lauren an alternate means of keeping warm in the frigid months of winter in K-ville.

But their passion did not last long. An unexpected interruption came from outside. Charles, who we know had been planning his own visit with Lauren, had arrived in K-ville just in time to see his love step inside Tent 5. "I'll wait a few minutes and let her get comfortable," he whispered to himself. He also wanted to be certain that Thomas hadn't forgotten his promise to wait around the residence hall for the package; Charles did not want him to unexpectedly show up to join Lauren in the tent. After about five minutes Charles's eagerness overcame his caution. Not wanting to betray his approach with footsteps, Charles crept toward the tent. But, as he drew closer, he began to hear soft voices coming from the shelter. Charles knew the shift schedule. He knew the person who had the tent shift before Lauren's, and in his excitement Charles had failed to realize that when the girl entered, no boy came out. Aware of Steven's playboy reputation, it didn't take Charles long to recognize the people and the actions taking place inside. "She must have told him that Tom wouldn't be coming," mumbled Charles. "Then that bastard must have stolen my prize. But he doesn't love her like I do. He's just using her. To him, she's a trophy . . . a stuffed head to mount on his wall. I would have given her the affection she deserves. I would have treated her like the goddess she is."

Swelling with heartbroken anger, Charles found a bucket that he filled with water and ice from the nearby gymnasium and dragged it out to Tent 5. With the stealth of a prowling kitten he unzipped the tent's flap and pulled it back to reveal the two lovers in the midst of their passion. Charles looked on for a moment, picturing himself in Steven's place amid the bed of sleeping bags. His legs should have been intertwined with hers. Her lips should have been pressed to his . . .

🖋 🖋 🖋

"AHEM. . . ." Our Host cleared his throat.

"Oh, right," said the Engineer. "I forgot . . . we have a fresh-man in this tent."

❧   ❧   ❧

CHARLES HADN'T BEEN standing long at the entrance before Steven felt the cold seeping into the tent through the open flap. He looked up to see Charles's embittered face. Embarrassed to have been caught in the act of cuckoldry, but relieved that Charles was at the door and not Thomas, Steven stood, a pair of thick wool socks his only clothing. "Oh, Charles, it's just you," he stuttered. "Um . . . I can explain this. You see, we were . . . uh . . . just . . ."

"Just trying to keep warm," added Lauren, who had pulled a sleeping bag tight around her chest.

"Exactly!" exclaimed Steven. "You see, she came out to re-lieve me after my shift, and I . . . uh . . . hadn't dressed properly. I had come down with hypothermia and, if the truth be told, Lauren was just trying to save my life."

"I'll show you hypothermia," yelled Charles as he tossed the bucket of ice water across Steven's unclothed body while Lauren cowered beneath a pile of sleeping bags. Mind you, the tem-perature was barely above freezing and there was a strong wind blowing, and here stood a naked man drenched in ice cold water. As you can imagine, Steven let out a scream that could be heard well beyond the group of tents nearby.

In his room, not very far away, Tom sat at his desk waiting

for a package that would never arrive. He heard the turmoil coming from outside. Between the scream, which could easily be mistaken for a siren, and the commotion created by such a loud noise, Tom assumed that a tent check had been called. He raced outside as fast as he could, not even remembering to bundle himself up in heavy clothes.

Meanwhile Charles had slipped away from the tent. Steven ran out screaming from the cold and his anger, leaving Lauren alone to dress hurriedly. Tom soon arrived, panting, cold, and curious. You can imagine his surprise when he found Lauren inside, but she wasted no time in making up an explanation for why she was in K-ville.

"My review session was canceled," she told him, "and I decided to come out here to keep you company. When I got here and no one was around, I thought it best to stay out here just in case they called a tent check and you were running late."

Thomas didn't have much time to consider this excuse, because Charles had come back with a second plan of attack. He knew he hadn't gotten Lauren with any of the water from the first bucket. His heart still aching with both rage and pain, he wanted revenge on her as well.

Charles stormed into the tent and tossed another bucket of water. He was, however, too blind with rage to realize that the person he was aiming at was not Lauren, but his friend Tom. The undeserving victim let out a scream not unlike Steven's. Once Charles recognized what he had done, he dropped the bucket and raced out of the tent. Tom chased after Charles for the remainder of the day and into the weekend, but was never able to catch up with him. You can just bet that from that day on Charles locked his door whenever he was in his room, and he snuck through the halls in order to avoid his angry neighbor. Worst of all, on account of the water incident, Charles knew that Tom would never believe a word of what he might try to tell him about Steven and Lauren. As for Steven, he convinced those who had seen him running naked through K-ville that he had done so as part of a fraternity prank.

And so the encounter between the two lovers ended with no consequences for them, except for Steven's ice-cold shower. Steven later deemed the frigid bath to be worth the trouble: in addition to his conquest in the tent, he was part of the fifth group let into Cameron Indoor Stadium for the big game against UNC.

THE SOCIOLOGY MAJOR

When the crowd in the tent had finished laughing at Thomas's, Charles's, and Steven's foolish behavior in their quest to win Lauren's heart, most agreed that it was an enjoyable tale of Krzyzewskiville. The only tenter who seemed distressed by the tale was the Sociology Major. Because the Engineer had mocked Thomas's sociology major so ruthlessly, he must have taken more offense at the Engineer's story than the other Trinity College tent members did.

"You know what?" asked the Sociology Major, waving around a half-empty bottle of beer, "I could easily counter your tale with the story of an engineering frat boy and his stupidity. But as a Trinity student, I have a little more common sense. I know that being vindictive has few rewards, so I'll rise above your juvenile criticism. I will, however, respond to your implications about my chosen major. In the case of you engineers, I daresay that no matter how difficult the problem, at least you can find the right answer. My work, on the other hand, is always subject to opinions and conditions. We have to constantly adapt to influences and changes. We have no definitive givens to work with except for the certainty of unpredictability, which looms over everything we attempt. In addition, you always claim that your degree will help you make money. I'll grant you my major may not be as lucrative, but at least I enjoy it.

"And you know what else," continued the Sociology Major, before he paused to gulp down the rest of his beer. He belched monstrously and then finished his statement. "Life isn't always about the amount of money you make, or the speed of your car, or the size of your house. If you're not happy with your occupation, nothing else you do matters nearly as much. Right now you may choose to ignore my admonitions. But I can assure you of one thing: although you might someday live in a larger house than I will, or drive a faster car, one day you'll be stuck in rush-hour traffic at eight o'clock in the morning, trying to get to that boring nine-to-five job. And you know what? That added horsepower under your hood won't be able to help you escape reality. When you're stuck in that traffic jam with nothing better to do than stare at the taillights in front of you, I hope your mind wanders to this conversation, and you think of me and whatever it is that I might be doing. You can be certain of this: I will be fulfilled by my career."

When the Sociology Major finished his treatise, our Host spoke up. "What's the purpose of all this wisdom?" he asked. "Why are you so set on wasting our time? We're here to tell stories about Krzyzewskiville, not to pontificate. You can preach about the supposed 'real world' of life after college all you want, but I'm the only person in this tent with the authority to speak on it. Now, if you don't mind, it's getting late. Your third personal check could soon come and interrupt our game, so please, tell your story or else please be quiet."

"Okay, everybody," said the Sociology Major, offended. "I'll just ask that no one get angry while I respond to this Engineer, and perhaps make a fool of him as well. It is, after all, perfectly legal to defend yourself when attacked."

HERE BEGINS THE
SOCIOLOGY MAJOR'S TALE

In the early '90s, tenting at Duke had become a more popular pastime than ever before. Of course, those were the years surrounding the school's first two NCAA basketball championships, and as you might expect, Craziness had reached a fever pitch. But in the mid-'90s, facilitated by a couple of substandard seasons for the Duke basketball team, the mythic grandeur that is K-ville began to fade. We know better than to worry that the end had come to the fledgling tenting tradition, however; after all, here we are tonight, telling stories in a tent in anticipation of a Duke victory over Carolina tomorrow.

In 1998, K-ville sprouted anew from the wintry ground and blossomed into a city like it had never been before. By the day of the Carolina game, more than a hundred tents were in line. The majority of these tents had been up for longer than six weeks. But an extremely rainy season, combined with an exceedingly lengthy tenting period, had made for one of the most loathed

56

K-ville experiences in this city's short history. As is often the case in the cold and wet season, sickness ran rampant among the students. And let's not forget where many of the students spent their days: the unhygienic nature of a tent city encouraged the spread of disease. K-ville began to look as though it had been struck by some pestilence: an onlooker might have thought he was witnessing a scene from Daniel Defoe's *A Journal of the Plague Year*.

The long wait did not discourage too many tenters; people had set up tents well in advance of games in years past. Despite the cold, most tenters were accustomed to dealing with the wintry weather, and, in the recesses of K-ville, fast-spreading illnesses have long been common occurrences. These three elements — duration, weather, and sickness — left most students unfazed. However, in 1998, the problems in Krzyzewskiville were complicated by the administration. A group of university officials began publicly expressing their concerns for security and student safety during the tenting period. They encouraged the student government to implement new regulations to deal with electric appliances, security, and alcoholic beverages.

What more could have gone wrong in 1998? Well, in addition to K-ville's usual problems, the new head line monitor brought the city into an era of political corruption. For our purposes I'll leave out his proper name — I'm not one to speak ill of another person, and besides, what if one of you knows him? — and instead will refer to him by a pseudonym: Roger.

Roger also happened to be an engineer. Perhaps his chosen

major suggests why he so poorly controlled Krzyzewskiville: after all, who wouldn't agree that engineers tend to lack proper social skills? I think our drunken friend here has proven that engineers aren't especially qualified to hold positions of authority. And engineers should never be allowed to govern a city, even one as small as the 1,300-person Krzyzewskiville.

THE SOCIOLOGY MAJOR'S STORY IS
INTERRUPTED BY THE HOST

"My friend," interrupted the Host, "I don't believe this is the right time to be making such claims. If indeed the words you have spoken are your beliefs, and let us hope they aren't, there's no need to speak them here. Right now, you're still angry. Surely you don't mean what you say. And if you do, we've no time for such petty quarrels. Engineers and Arts and Sciences students have been arguing for years. One school is not better than the other, nor is one group of majors more useful. A degree in music will not be very helpful to a biomedical engineer, but if you intend to be a musician, then there's likely no better major. Now, with that settled, get on with it. Tell us your story and we'll form our own opinions about engineers."

"You're right," answered the Sociology Major, "I have digressed." He pointed to the Engineer and said, "I've let my rage bring me to his level! There's no need for me to personally insult him: my tale will speak to the character of engineers in general." He adjusted his collar, glanced again toward the engineer, and then said, "It's time for me to get on with my story." The Sociology Major took a long, calming breath and resumed his tale.

THE SOCIOLOGY MAJOR'S
STORY CONTINUES

Roger's abilities should have come under question for other reasons besides his leadership skills. He had no past experience monitoring the tents. Although a prior term as a line monitor is not required to be chosen as the head line monitor, Roger's lack of experience made him prone to mistakes concerning some of the simplest aspects of the tenting process. The checks he held were chaotic, and no one knew where to report. I heard that he once called a check while nobody was in K-ville because they had just been given a grace period. This might remind some of you of the 2002–2003 tenting season, when a head line monitor with little tenting experience was chosen because of his connections. However, I'll let someone else tell that story; I'm certain that it's one we'll want to hear.

Lack of experience was not the only problem for Roger that year in K-ville. I believe it was Lord Acton who once said "Power tends to corrupt, and absolute power corrupts absolutely. Great men are almost always bad men. . . . There is no worse heresy than that the office sanctifies the holder of it." Krzyzewskiville is a city, and its leader holds a position of power — so why should he be any less susceptible to human nature? Roger's power over

59

this city led to a corruption that nearly destroyed the tenting tradition.

I've already explained that there were more than a hundred tents set up for the games, and because the first tent was pitched extremely early, K-ville grew unusually quickly. The Duke team was wildly popular in 1998, and K-ville and Cameron weren't large enough to accommodate the number of students willing to tent for the game. A corrupt—and apparently addicted—leader was dangerous, given the competition for admission to the games.

"Are you up for some poker tonight?" asked one of Roger's fraternity brothers.

"Of course. You know I always am," answered Roger, who was rumored to have a gambling problem. "When and where?"

"Meet us at ten o'clock in the commons room. Make sure you bring plenty of money to lose."

Roger laughed and said, "I'll be bringing money, but I don't plan on losing any of it. In fact, I think it'll be the money I won from you last week."

Around ten o'clock that night Roger entered his fraternity's commons room. In the middle of the room was a circular table with six chairs. Five of them were filled, and Roger took his seat at the sixth place. In front of him had already been set a stack of chips. "What's the buy-in tonight?" he asked, noticing that the stack seemed taller than normal.

"We're starting at fifty dollars," said one of the players. "Is that too much for you, Roger?"

"Not at all," he replied. "That just means that there's more money for me to win."

The players were dealt their first five cards. Unbeknownst to Roger, the full house he held was not a sign of his good fortune. But with it, he convincingly won the first hand and was up ten dollars already. "Just a continuation of where we left off last week, gentlemen," gloated Roger as he raked in the chips. "And, if I remember correctly, it's also a continuation of the week before." Roger had won the two weeks prior, though not for the same lofty stakes. He didn't know that his two previous victories had been planned as well.

It took ten hands before the first person had been knocked out of the game. But soon thereafter they fell fast until only Roger and one other frat brother were left. Both players had nearly the same number of chips. On the last hand of the night, Roger was holding a straight flush to the six with all of his money in the pot. The other player matched the bet, and then said "Let's make this worthwhile."

"Worthwhile? How?" Roger asked.

"I'll raise you five hundred dollars," answered his friend.

Roger knew he didn't have enough money to cover that, but he also knew that he was holding a nearly unbeatable hand. He hesitated a few moments while he stared at the progression of hearts fanned between his fingers. "Why not?" he said, trying to sound confident and relaxed. "It's only money, right? You're on. I'll see your bet, and I'll call."

Roger's opponent revealed his hand one card at a time. The

six of spades dropped onto the wooden table. When the seven of spades followed, Roger began to feel concerned. "It's okay," he told himself, "the first cards of his straight might just happen to be of the same suit." Roger repeated this thought for both the eight of spades and the nine. When the ten of spades had been tossed onto the pile, Roger knew he had lost.

"I don't believe it," muttered Roger as he set his cards face down on the table. "What are the chances of you beating a straight flush to the six?"

The onlookers began to laugh and taunt. Their voices seemed distant to Roger. "Man . . . that really hurts," said one. "Get ready to pay up; you owe some big money," jeered another.

As for Roger, he sat at the table and stared at his cards. Occasionally he would mumble, "How did I lose?"

"I would prefer cash, but I guess I can take a check from you," said his friend who had won the game. "But remember, I'll be charging you extra if it bounces."

Roger looked up and said, "I can't afford to give you that much money."

"What do you mean you can't afford it?" asked his friend. "Then why did you bet it?"

"I . . . I don't know. I didn't think I could lose."

"Well you did, so you better pay up."

"Hey, I know what you can do," interrupted one of the other brothers, on cue. "Why don't you work out a trade?"

"What kind of trade?" asked Roger. "I don't have anything to give you."

"What do you mean? You're the head line monitor. You can get him into the Carolina game without making him tent."

"You're right," said Roger, as beads of sweat began to roll across his forehead. "I can do that. Would you be willing to take that as a trade?"

"Not for five hundred dollars," answered the victor. "I don't think not having to tent is worth that much. How about you get all of us in, then we'll call it even."

"But I don't know if I can. I mean, how would I do that?"

"I don't know. So I guess you'd better muster five hundred dollars."

"Actually," chimed another bystander, "Five hundred and fifty dollars. You forgot about his original buy-in."

That night, Tent 31-A was created, at least on paper, in order to accommodate the group of Roger's fraternity brothers that would be attending the Carolina game. But secrets are not well kept among a large group of friends. Other brothers in the frat learned of the special "fake tent," and they wanted to get in. More tricks were played on Roger, and more bargains were made. Rumor has it that the occupancy of Tent 31-A had reached thirty by the day of the Carolina game. That means thirty students from an already overcrowded K-ville would not be able to get into Cameron despite the many days they had spent waiting in a tent.

Game time came, and the students lined up alongside K-ville. In the middle of the queue were the thirty non-tenting students. Roger opened the doors and began letting students inside. However, when the members of Tent 1 entered the arena, a group of students had already taken seats on the TV side. You see, the creation of Tent 31-A had not been the head line monitor's only corrupt action. Some students had bribed Roger to sneak them in before the doors opened. From what I've been told, a common device for this purpose had something to do with Roger's affinity for drugs. And if not drugs, it is said that sex worked well too. Of course, plain old-fashioned cash could buy a seat or, if need be, erase a missed tent check.

Imagine that you're in Tent 1. You've been sleeping outside since before the new year began during a particularly cold and rainy tenting season. When, at last, the doors of Cameron open, you expect to be the first person inside. What would you do if you saw a group of students already sitting in your hard-earned spot?

Although angry, the people who made it into the game did not create the commotion. Or if they did, it went unnoticed next to the near riot outside the stadium, where students who were not let into Cameron after having tented for weeks were understandably outraged. The campus police had to stop the left-out Crazies from getting destructive or violent.

The events of the 1998 tenting season, along with the administration's growing concerns for the safety and health of tenting students, nearly brought Krzyzewskiville to extinction. Since K-ville is still here today, you might be wondering what happened. Well, thanks to a compromise suggested by Dean Sue Wasiolek, the tenters who were left outside of Cameron were given free tickets and transportation to watch the Blue Devils play in the ACC tournament, held in Greensboro that year. Also, underclassmen who had tented but not made it into Cameron were guaranteed admission into the Carolina game the next year without having to go through the tenting process.

But appeasing the disgruntled tenters would not solve all of K-ville's problems. The administration, still on the verge of putting an end to the young tradition, forced the student government to make a choice: they could either reorganize the city, or it would be shut down. In response, a new tenting policy was created to mollify university officials. It included many of the procedures, regulations, and guidelines that we follow today. The new policy also represented the first substantial instance of administrative interference into the affairs of the tenting students.

Although the city had been saved from extinction, we can never forget what events nearly led to the end of Krzyzewski-ville. Corruption, disorganization, and cronyism created outrage among students and the administration alike—and all the problems had been created by the irresponsibility of none other than an engineer.

THE PUBLIC POLICY MAJOR

When our friend the Sociology Major finished his story, we all looked toward the Engineer for his response. Much to our disappointment, there was none: the Engineer had heard scarcely a word. I would blame it on his excessive intake of beer. His head was still sagging across his girlfriend's lap, but now, his eyes were closed, and his breathing had grown even and shallow. The Sociology Major, however, paid no attention. Instead, he crossed his arms over his chest, laughed, and said, "Now, who dares tell a story in response to that?"

While other tenters whispered to one another the Public Policy Major chose to accept the Sociology Major's challenge. Her blue eyes focused on his smug face, and she began to contradict the history he had just endeavored to create. "I have to admit that your story was entertaining, but I must also suggest that your account was somewhat biased. From the stories I've been told—and mind you, my brother was a student here at that time—the engineer was not the only head line monitor that year. Two men were appointed, for reasons I'm unsure of, and the other, to the best of my knowledge, was in Trinity College."

Since the dozing Engineer was the Public Policy Major's boyfriend, we can assume that she felt obliged to defend him. Our Host seemed to recognize this logic as well and decided to include a comment of his own before letting her proceed. "I'll have to give you credit," he said. "It must be hard to defend your drunken boyfriend who is making a fool of himself as we speak. Look! There's drool dangling from his mouth while he sleeps!" Everyone in the tent had a good laugh at these words, save, of course, the drunken and now snoring Engineer. But despite his jeering, the Host was also quick to admit the truth behind the Public Policy Major's statement, saying, "However, I'll also acknowledge that you're right—the story we just heard was not entirely accurate. According to some of the research that I have already done, there were two head line monitors in K-ville that tenting season. The story can be attributed to either of them. And from what I can tell, our good Sociology Major skipped over some other details. It's hard to separate fact and fiction about that year's events in K-ville. As a journalist, I know that stories can often be embellished, particularly when a teller wants to romanticize a series of events for his audience. Even I find myself aggrandizing the episodes of my college career. I can't always remember which experiences I've inflated and which events actually happened.

"In my research, I've come across stories of near-riots on campus as a result of the line monitors' debacles. These people remember police with riot gear turning fire hoses onto students forming human blockades. Fires were lit all over campus, and just about anything not bolted down was burned. And supposedly, these episodes lasted for three or four days.

"However, I've also heard other retellings of the events of that evening. Some people will tell you that the students were angry, but quickly pacified by appeasing administrators and line monitors. Given these discrepancies, let's avoid another story about this bad moment in Krzyzewskiville's past. If your curiosity continues, I suggest asking a member of that year's K-ville what happened on the night of the Carolina game. But don't count on getting an entirely factual account."

As for myself, I have heard rumors of other events from 1998. But I too am unable to distinguish between the myths and the true events. Let this just be a lesson that stories, certainly those about a tradition with little written history, are easily and often embellished. Do not believe every word you hear (and perhaps you should be wary of the words you read as well).

After our Host quieted the individual conversations among the tenters, he returned his gaze to the Public Policy Major. While our conversation had drifted, she had used the edge of her coat sleeve to wipe the saliva from her boyfriend's mouth. "Now, since you have already spoken out," said the Host, "and the ordering by seniority has gone awry, let's go ahead and hear your story if you are prepared with one to tell."

"Well," said the Public Policy Major before a slight hesitation to brush a few strands of pale hair from her eyes, "I suppose

I can practically continue where the last story left off. We were just told of a year during which my brother was a tenter. The administration's requirement to establish new rules in Krzyzewskiville forced a change in the way students went about tenting, setting a new standard for the 'die-hard' fan. My brother, Will, was one of those devoted tenters, and I suppose I can tell all of you about one of his experiences in Krzyzewskiville."

"Great," exclaimed the Sociology Major, "but don't you think it would be better to wake him first?" He pointed to the still-snoring Engineer. "It would be a shame for him to drown in a puddle of his own drool!" He laughed snidely while I and the other tenters watched in silence, waiting for the Public Policy Major's reaction.

Her icy blue eyes fixed themselves on the jeering Sociology Major until his laughing had tapered into little more than heavy breathing. A crease of a smile appeared in the folds of her cheeks before she responded, "I don't think so. It will be easier without his slurred ramblings interrupting my tale. Just promise to leave him be!" She then moved on to the story about her brother's experiences in K-ville.

HERE BEGINS THE PUBLIC
POLICY MAJOR'S TALE

Besides bringing the disappointment of a bitter end without a third national championship, the 1997–98 basketball season sparked the Renaissance of Krzyzewskiville. The tent city reappeared amid controversy and corruption, tribulations that did nothing to deter its citizens. The next year brought the Crazies out as usual, but the rules had changed. K-ville was growing into a city requiring strict governance.

Most of us here would not recognize the tenting system before the 1998–99 basketball season. The undervalued organization, monitoring, and convoluted tenting policies that have become synonymous with K-ville, though often maligned and criticized by students, were, before the 1998–99 tenting season, inconsistent and disorganized. K-ville wasn't in anarchy, but it was in chaos. Concerned that a student might be injured or that the length of tenting might hinder academic pursuits, the administration decided it was time either to end the tradition of the tent city or to require stricter regulations.

Two students were charged with the task of redefining the tenting policy so that tenters could wait for basketball games in an orderly and safe manner. Their task also included maintaining the tradition of equity that had always existed in K-ville, and the most important priority was to maintain the integrity of the line. People often neglect the fact that tenting, though romanticized by the media, has but one true purpose. Krzyzewskiville is, after all, simply a line—albeit a famous one. The first person in the line is, rightfully, the first person inside Cameron. The previous year, this primary purpose of the line had been neglected, but the new system would need to guarantee a tenter's place. Come game time in years past, the students would surround the doors to Cameron as they shoved and jockeyed for position. There was once even an instance when so many students attempted to push their way inside that the doors to the stadium broke off their hinges. Never again would such an event happen. The monitoring would better control the flow of students. Numbered wristbands designed to mark a student's exact position in line were implemented so that monitors could track the order of the students' admission into a game.

The administration's preeminent concern regarding Krzyzewskiville was for the students' safety. Tenting provides an ideal setting for a catastrophic accident. Crime, disease, fires, and hypothermia are just some of the dangers confronting students who tent. Before the administration intervened, some surprising "amenities" could be found in the tent city. Take, for example, the presence of fire. The area surrounding more than a hundred canvas tents is not the best place for open flames. But the months of January and February are quite cold, and I daresay the prospect of being warm clouds a person's logic. Just as you might see on the streets of another city, K-ville once sported barrels blazing with a warming fire. My brother told me of an instance when Coach K had appeared in K-ville with a truckload of firewood. "Rough practice," was all he said as he presented the wood he had just chopped to release his frustration. Today fires are not permitted, and instead we try to stay warm with blankets.

Some other common sights in and around the tents were electrical cords running from the basements of Card Gym and Cameron. Students used to bring televisions, game systems, and space heaters to their tents, but no longer. In order to prevent the possibility of an electrical fire, the Durham fire marshal will occasionally patrol the town and make sure no one is using outlet-powered equipment. Another common amenity of K-ville was an ever-present supply of alcohol. Not to say that it can't be found today, as my boyfriend has proven, but in years past, kegs were more common than hot chocolate. After all, who needs heat when you're too drunk to realize you're cold? Alcohol is not banned these days, but kegs are certainly frowned upon. On the other hand, we are college kids, and alcohol is often a part of the college experience.

I guess K-ville was once a little more comfortable, but then again, today we don't even need power cords to run our computers as we sit in our tents. Besides, we can always plug into the Ethernet jacks in the lampposts. Did you know the university spent $40,000 installing those, in addition to the wireless network we also have out here? We don't have to worry too much about our laptops — or anything else — randomly catching fire now, so I suppose the new regulations are probably for the best.

Now, to get on with my story, what was probably the single most significant aspect of the new policy was the decision that no tent could be set up more than ten days in advance of a game. Any tent found in place before that would be taken down by the line monitors and university police. And in addition to the restrictions on when tents could be set up, the new policy from the student government changed the limit on the number of members per tent from ten to twelve.

I bet what you're expecting is the story of the mad rush that took place ten days before the UNC game. But that's not what happened; instead, the establishment of K-ville that season took a unique turn. Duke students, both intelligent and profoundly fanatical about their basketball, devised a way around the letter of the law.

In recent years, tenting had been limited to two predetermined games a year and has always begun after the winter break. But in November 1998, excitement about the basketball season had already begun to pervade the gothic wonderland. Expectations were high after Duke, ranked number one in the country, had routed some of its early opponents. Duke's domination of teams from Fairfield University and South Carolina State drew a crowd of Crazies out to K-ville in November. My brother William, along with two other members of his tent and, of course, various other tenters, cut short their Thanksgiving break in order to register a tent and set up camp for the upcoming games against Florida and Michigan. On the Saturday following Thanksgiving, Tent 4 had officially been registered, and my brother and his friends, Jared and Marcus, spent their first night in K-ville.

Jared had brought a small charcoal grill from home, and the three tenters sat on an open sleeping bag outside of the tent cooking food and chatting. "I can't believe we're Tent 4," Marcus said. "Our seats should be right in front."

"I'm surprised more people didn't come back early," responded my brother, "but I'm sure they'll show up tomorrow."

Jared looked up from the browning hamburgers and said, "Who cares, as long as we get in before them."

"After last year's fiasco," added Marcus, "I wouldn't be so certain."

Jared laughed in agreement, but William stared at the smoldering charcoal in silence. Marcus noticed his friend's distraction and asked, "What's wrong, Will? Aren't you excited about our spot?"

"Of course I am," William explained, "but there's still something bothering me. With this new tenting policy, how are we supposed to regularly guarantee ourselves a good spot in line?"

After a minute or so of thought, Jared said, "I'm not sure if I see why you're worried. We're already Tent 4."

"I don't think you understand the problem, Jared," answered William. "I don't mind setting up the tent early. After all, if we want a good seat, we should be willing to dedicate more time to the tenting process. But with this new ten-day limit, how can we guarantee ourselves good seats for the other games? Think about it. Who wouldn't be willing to spend ten days camping to be in the front row of Cameron? But the person who is willing to spend two months is more deserving of the better seats. This distinction can't happen with the policy as it's written. The more dedicated fans have just as much of a chance of being in a low-numbered tent as the less committed ones."

"I guess I never thought about that," answered Jared. "But that's a good point. Who's to say we'll get to the tent registration desk first?"

"I don't know," said William. "We'll have to figure out how to be the first ones in line to register our tent with the line monitors. We'll need to station people all over campus so that when they announce the secret location for tent registration, a representative from our tent will be nearby."

In case you were wondering, both the Florida game on December 9 and the Michigan game three days later were nothing short of blowouts. Against the Gators, Will Avery had 26 points and 9 assists while hitting a Duke record of 8 three-pointers. The final score was 116–86. Next, the Devils went on to avenge two straight losses to the Wolverines. Trajan Langdon's 7 three-pointers—which helped him to surpass the school's previous three-pointer career record—pushed the score to 102–55 when the walk-ons entered the game. The final outcome was Duke over Michigan, 108–64. After these two victories, Krzyzewskiville closed for the year. The tents were taken down, and members of Tent 4, along with the other students, took their finals and went home for winter break.

William left school still pondering the problem of his tent number. I can still remember him discussing it with my parents, both Duke alums, at the dinner table. "You know, honey, there's really not a bad seat in Cameron," my mom reasoned as she ladled a spoonful of gravy atop my brother's mashed potatoes. "Does it really matter if you're not in the first row of the student section? We never had tenting, or any of that foolish stuff. We got to the games when they started, and we could always see the court just fine."

"That's not the point," argued my brother. "Of course we can watch the game from anywhere. Heck, if it was just about a good view of the game, then I would stay home and watch it on TV."

"So why don't you do that?" I asked. Now, don't laugh. This was before I had seen a game in person in Cameron.

"You don't understand," my brother tried to explain. "Sitting in the student section is part of what makes the games so exciting. It's about being there with my classmates, screaming and jumping. It's about being able to disrupt the concentration of the opponent to help our team win. It's about giving a high-five to the stranger standing next to me every time Trajan sinks a three."

At this point, my dad interjected. He turned to me and said, "Trust me, Katherine, if you decide to go to Duke, you'll understand." He took a long drink from the glass of iced tea in his hand, set it down on the wooden table, and spoke again. "Now, William, tell me again why you can't pitch your tent any earlier than ten days before the game?"

"Just like I've told you, Dad, the line monitors will take it down. The tent policy specifically states that you can't set up a tent more than ten days prior to a game. We have to register at the same time as everyone else, which means if we don't find the secret registration desk early, then we don't get a good spot in line."

I remember seeing the look of a brilliant idea flash in the depths of my father's brown eyes. He was silent for a few minutes while he mulled it over. After another swig of iced tea he spoke again, saying, "Well, what if you don't set up a tent?"

"We've thought about that," responded my brother. "But how long can we stay out there without any kind of shelter? It gets really cold, especially at night. And what would we do if it rains? Besides, I'm sure other people have already come up with the same idea."

My dad smiled and shook his head. "No, that's not what I meant. And remember, I'm your father. I wouldn't encourage my son to sleep outside for a week in the middle of January without any sort of shelter. But, if the policy specifically says that you can't set up a tent, what's to stop you from setting up some *other* form of shelter?"

I remember watching my brother stare at my father. It must have taken him a few moments to understand the idea. Then, he virtually leapt from his chair and ran upstairs. He came down a minute later waving a copy of the tenting policy and exclaiming, "You're right, Dad, it only says you can't set up a tent."

My brother went back to school with a big, blue tarp in his trunk. He and his friends had decided that instead of tenting they would "tarp." You see, there used to be a chain-link fence running along the edge of the sidewalk near Cameron. My brother and his tent staked one side of the tarp into the ground and then tied the other side to the top of the fence. Thus, "tarping" was contrived. And although no "tent" was first in line, my brother and his friends bypassed the need to register by devising another way to line up outside the stadium. Not to be beaten into the stadium, the other Crazies saw the new structure and followed the same plan. Before a couple of days had passed, the tent city had become a tarp village, until ten days prior to the game when my brother and his friends took down Tarp 1, and erected Tent 1 in its place.

THE PUBLIC POLICY MAJOR
CONTINUES WITH AN EPILOGUE
TO HER TALE

"Technically, my brother and his friends followed the rules to the letter. They did not set up a tent until ten days before the game. Instead, they surrounded themselves with chain-link fence and a flimsy blue canvas. Now, if you think it's cold inside this tent, imagine not being protected from the wind on all sides. The tarps were no more than miniature wind tunnels that did nothing except help the Crazies ward off the rain. Yet, as I've told you, as soon as that first tarp began the line, hundreds of other tarpers made camp nearby in the same makeshift fashion until ten days before the first game when the students were finally allowed to officially raise tents."

"I'll bet those students developed more of an appreciation for the shelter of a tent," suggested the Pre-Law student.

"I'm sure they did," replied the Public Policy Major, "and I think staying under the tarps proved the true dedication of the fans. These students have a passion for their team that can't be hampered by rules or by weather. But, more important, and what you've all hopefully seen, is the problem with a time regulation in the tenting policy. Most of the Crazies would be willing to have a tent rotation for ten days in order to be in the front row of Cameron. If a maximum to the tenting period is set, then the purpose of K-ville is no longer as important. If K-ville exists for the most dedicated fans to get the best seats at the game, then what happens when the university places a maximum on dedication? But in tarping, Duke fans proved their loyalty, with the most dedicated fans making more sacrifices simply to get into the games."

"I have a question," interjected the Host as he chewed on the end of his pen. "If this time-limit solution didn't work, how does the school keep the tenting period in check? What's to stop a student from setting up a tent on the first day of school in the fall?"

"Technically . . ." said the Public Policy Major, before trailing off. She thought for a moment, and then said, "I suppose nothing is really stopping anyone from setting up tents before Christmas, except for some degree of sanity. However, in response to tarping as a new measure of dedication, the student government had to amend the guidelines for tenting. We owe the creation of the blue- and white-tenting periods to people like my brother who refused to submit to restrictions on their Craziness. Stricter guidelines for earlier tenting help to reduce the length of a given tenting period. But despite the other changes and regulations that Krzyzewskiville faced during the 1998–99 tenting campaign, at least we know that tenting still serves its primary purpose. K-ville admits students into the games in order of their dedication, which, in turn, ensures the quality of the fans in Cameron."

THE FRESHMAN

"Very interesting!" exclaimed our Host when the Public Policy Major had completed her history of tarping and her explanation of why certain regulations are destructive. "I'd never heard this story before. I'm sure you're all extremely happy that William and his friends were the ones who went through tarping instead of you. And can you picture the mad rush of students all trying to set up camp on the same afternoon ten days before a game? Worse yet, what would happen if the most enthusiastic fans found themselves in the back of the stadium staring down at the less enthusiastic fans crowding the front rows simply because they decided that they could bear to camp out for ten days?"

"I'm glad there aren't a maximum number of days for tenting. I think you should have to show more dedication to earn a better place inside Cameron." These words of agreement came from our Captain's younger brother. Admittedly, this comment was unexpected—not so much because of what he said, but because he said anything at all. Not only was he a freshman whom none of us knew well, but I can scarcely recall an occasion on which I had heard this tenter say more than "hello," except when he echoed the words of his brother.

"Why do you say that?" asked the Host. "I can't think of another school where students need to wait in line for ten days just to get inside their stadium. It's my impression that ten days would certainly be sufficient to earn admission to a game, even if it weren't for the best seats in the house."

"Well . . ." stuttered the Freshman as he recognized that his outburst had forced him into the conversation, "it seems to me that being able to see a Duke basketball game inside Cameron Indoor Stadium is an opportunity few people get. I checked the prices of tickets online once, just out of curiosity. A pair of seats to the NC State game were selling for more than $1,000 at auction. And an auction is pretty much the only way to get tickets because Cameron has been sold out since . . . well . . . who knows when? I wonder if I had even been born before the last time a ticket was available at the box office for a game played while students weren't on break."

By this time, the Economics Major was frowning. She snapped the question, "So, you think money should represent our dedication to the basketball program? You're only proving how naive freshmen are."

The Freshman, recoiling at the criticism, stammered a further explanation. "No, it's not just money or the availability of tickets. Keep in mind that you're at Duke, and you'll never have this chance again. Camping out in Krzyzewskiville is part of being at this university. No other school has a tent city, but many know of it and try to emulate it. Just the other day I overheard the head line monitor talking about a student at another university contacting him to ask for the K-ville rules and regulations. That other school wants to create their own K-ville. What they don't understand is that this experience is about more than just a set of rules, it's about interactions.

"One of the reasons I came to this university was because of the anecdotes I had heard from my brother. He'd come home during breaks and tell us all the stories about the past year's K-ville, but he doesn't talk about the tent policy. He talks about the other members of his tent, the events, the controversies, the parties and, of course, the basketball games. Once I heard all of those stories, I knew there was no place I would rather be.

"Have you ever noticed that when someone asks where you go to school, and you say Duke, the first thing you almost always hear is 'Oh, great basketball.' That's what Duke is. Of course this school has everything else as well. The academics, the campus, and the people are all incredible. But Duke basketball is a household name. Tenting is a part of that Duke basketball tradition. We have to be true to it or else we're destroying the integrity of the system! Ten days isn't nearly enough time for someone to prove their devotion, and it certainly doesn't merit the best seats inside Cameron."

As you might imagine, these words caused quite a stir from the tenting veterans. Some agreed, while others simply laughed at him for showing such strong opinions based on such little experience. In the interest of our contest, the Host was quick to quiet everyone down. He was unsure of how much longer the group would have until the last personal check was called. "Quiet, everyone!" he exclaimed. "I know very well that nobody will want to stay around for more stories once your camping requirements are complete, with the exception, perhaps, of this lone Freshman, who seems to feel that people should have to do more in order to fulfill the true purpose of tenting.

"Everyone deserves an opinion. In all fairness, I believe that we should let this boy speak. After all, he's spent as many weeks outside this year as any of you. In that time I imagine he has learned a thing or two about tenting. From these experiences, let him explain why he thinks more time should be spent outside."

Realizing he still had to tell a story, the Freshman decided on his course of action. "If none of you mind, I'll address your criticisms and tell my tale at the same time, because I'll use my story to tell of the importance of spending time in K-ville."

The other group members agreed to listen to what this novice tenter had to say and quieted themselves enough to hear the hesitant breaths of the Captain's younger brother. The increasingly nervous Freshman did not say a word for almost a minute. At last, he cleared his throat and started his tale. I will now recount it for you here.

Imagine with me, if you will, a method for distributing tickets to basketball games that's unlike the K-ville line system. Imagine a lottery structure akin to what other schools use. I give you Maryland as my first example. From what I've heard, Maryland students get their tickets by registering online for a lottery system. Carolina uses a lottery too, meaning dedication does not guarantee you seats inside of the stadium—not that anyone could really enjoy a game inside the Dean Dome, that monstrosity of an arena. There is, of course, one inherent flaw in the lottery method. It does not guarantee a student the chance to see a game. Now I'll grant you that the likelihood of a Maryland or Carolina student never being able to get a ticket to any game is quite slim. But to get into a major game, perhaps against a rival such as Duke . . . well, that could be wishful thinking, especially for a freshman.

Here at Duke the system is perfect. No matter how important a game is, or how much you hate the rival, if you want to see the team play in person, you're guaranteed a spot—so long as you're willing to pay the price, and a small one at that, of waiting in line until the game starts. With our system, luck isn't a factor, and it shouldn't be. Luck is not what proves your dedication to the team.

The best way to explain the purpose of the system is to look at the population of K-ville. More tenters are here from the freshman class than from any other. Logically speaking, this phenomenon doesn't make much sense. Because they live on East Campus, the freshmen are housed furthest from Cameron. Yet, first-year students comprise the greatest per-class population for the tenting basketball games. This statistic proves that the freshmen are the more dedicated fans. Remember that when the line monitors call an hour grace period after a tent check, all of you can go back to your warm rooms. But what about us freshmen? Most of that hour would be taken up going to and from East Campus. And when tenting is graced for the night, the freshmen are the kids who often aren't able to make it back to their rooms because the buses have stopped running, forcing us to spend the night out in K-ville whether we're required to or not.

On the other hand, perhaps there's a senior living very near to Cameron who has grown complacent with Duke's winning. You hear it all the time: "Oh, we're playing *so and so*. We should beat them," or "That's not an important game." And the team doesn't make it to the Final Four, so it was a bad season despite a 25–6 record and having won the ACC tournament and made it to the Sweet Sixteen. This person won't take the time out of his day to go watch Duke battle an unranked team simply because Duke "should win." Of course, this senior would certainly want to go watch the UNC game because that's the biggest game of the year. That's the game where everyone shows up and they paint themselves blue and wear crazy outfits. That's the game the media talks about. That's the game where the press will be.

But this senior won't bother to walk across the street to see a "less important" game. Why would this person deserve good seats, or any seats at all, simply because he was lucky enough to have his number called?

Let me tell you about a conversation I overheard toward the end of last semester. I was waiting for my American history class to begin when I overheard two guys in front of me talking about tenting. One of them, I think his name was Brandon, was asking his friend when he wanted to start tenting.

"So, Todd," began Brandon, "when do you want to set up the tent for next semester? Since the games are so late next year, I don't suppose we'll have to get back from vacation early. If we set up when classes start, we should have a pretty good tent number."

Todd avoided turning toward Brandon to answer. Instead, he stared down at his notebook, saying, "I don't think I want to tent this year."

"What do you mean you don't want to tent?" asked Brandon. He watched the back of Todd's head because his friend refused to look up.

"I . . . I just don't think I'll have the time this year. My classes will be too hard. I won't be able to get my homework done."

"Not get your homework done? Are you kidding me? Since when have you done all of your homework?" Todd finally looked up when Brandon made that condescending remark, so he quickly added, "I'm just joking. But really, you know it's easier to get work done in the tent than in your room. Out there you have nothing better to do. In your room there are so many distractions that it takes twice as long to finish the same amount of homework . . ." Brandon paused and looked down at the newspaper on his desk. Then he mumbled, "that is, if your fingers don't freeze off."

Todd rolled his eyes as he turned his head back toward his notes. Then he said, "It's not just work. I don't think all that waiting is worth it just for a good seat. I can see the game much better on television. Why spend all that time in the cold? You get into Cameron and you wind up having to watch the game standing up, crammed next to the people around you and you have to constantly scream. That just doesn't seem worth it when I can sit in my room where it's easier to watch the game, order a pizza and lie on the couch. Besides, a true fan would rather be able to watch the entire game. You can't see everything if you're standing behind some tall guy or you're shoved into a corner of the student section."

"Give me a break," sighed an exasperated Brandon. "You would rather watch the game on television because it's easier to see? First of all, you know as well as I do that there are no bad seats in Cameron. Besides, it's just as likely that you'll miss something while trying to watch a game on TV. You can't control the camera. For instance, remember that streaker during the Carolina game? I'm sure ESPN didn't show that on television."

"True," answered Todd as a small smile crossed his face. "But then again, maybe I didn't want to see that."

Brandon shrugged and nodded his head to suggest that perhaps Todd had made a valid point. But he continued arguing, "And don't try to tell me you're more of a fan because you want to see the entire game on television. A good fan would want to show up to every game and be as loud as he possibly could in order to disturb the concentration of the other team and help us win. That's why we're called the 'sixth man.' We're part of the team, and we help the team win."

Todd shook his head and mumbled, "I just can't tent this semester. I don't have the time."

After a few minutes of silence between the two friends, Brandon leaned back over toward Todd and said, "Okay, if you don't want to tent, I have a friend who's an RA. He has tickets in the buffer zone around the opponent's bench for the UNC game. He can't go so he offered me one of them. But if you want it, you can have it. I would rather tent."

Todd looked up, and without hesitation said, "Definitely! I'll take it."

Brandon laughed loudly enough to disturb the other students in the nearby rows, then he quieted himself until everyone stopped watching him. "What's so funny?" asked Todd.

"My friend's not really giving up his ticket. I just wanted to prove that you're too lazy to tent and that your reasons are nothing more than excuses."

Now you've heard about the conversation between Todd and Brandon. Would you want a person like Todd to have a better seat than you simply because luck helped him to a higher lottery number, although you would have been willing to demonstrate weeks or months worth of dedication to the team? Of course not! With the system we have now, the people who pay the price receive the preferred seats. What better way to run ticket distribution?

As luck would have it, I ran across Brandon and Todd once early this semester while they were eating lunch. Sitting at the table next to them, I overheard their conversation. I presume Brandon had persuaded Todd to tent since the latter was now complaining about problems in K-ville.

"Damn, it's cold," groaned Todd while he unwrapped the scarf from around his neck. "I can't believe they're still making us stay out there in this kind of weather. We should get some sort of grace period."

"It could be worse," answered Brandon, "at least it's sunny and dry. At this time last year K-ville was covered in rain, snow, or ice."

"But at least we got grace periods last year. This year's line monitors don't care at all about how much time we spend out there. Why should they, I suppose. They only have to come out once every few hours to do a tent check. If one of them had to stay out there with us, they would sympathize better with the plight of the common tenter."

Brandon rolled his eyes and said, "Thank you, Herr Marx. Perhaps we should stir up a revolution of the tenting proletariat and overthrow the tyrannical line monitor regime." He picked up his hamburger and took a bite.

But Todd wasn't finished complaining. He used Brandon's

joke to further chide the K-ville ruling elite. "You're damn right we should!" he agreed. "The line monitors are so disorganized that you'd think they'd never spent a night in a tent. They have no clue how to run a check. They just say your name once and if you don't answer that second they consider it a miss. Don't they know that it takes time to get out of the tent? I have to put on twenty different layers just to open the flap. Even with all of that on I can barely feel my hands."

Todd continued complaining throughout lunch, though I can't remember everything he said. My interest waned as much as Brandon's. I've added this last part to my story for a specific reason. I hate those people like Todd who choose to tent but can't stop whining. These students hardly deserve admission to the games. If they could, they would rather arrive at games and walk straight in. And tenting this year was easy. We've been given an unnecessary number of graces all season long for supposed inclement weather. What do people expect in January and February? Of course it'll be cold. You're planning on spending hours in a tent—be prepared for it! Don't come out to your tent in jeans and a t-shirt and expect to stay warm. Layer your clothes! Go buy some thermal underwear.

These complainers ruin the integrity of the line. What's the point of a line that you never have to be in unless the situation is ideal? Are those people who only tent in perfect weather proving their dedication? Are they deserving of admission? I suppose they've at least done a little more work than students who win a lottery, but still, hard-core tenting is about sacrificing for your tent and your team. If you aren't willing to sacrifice for the team, and give an adequate amount of effort, then just go home. Heck, that's what the walk-up line is for.

If I'm ever the head line monitor, I don't plan to be so lenient. Suffering and sacrificing is part of tenting. We're the Cameron Crazies and the world expects us to do crazy, and even stupid, things to get into games. But we're becoming spoiled by the lax nature of the line. If this continues, we might as well do away with the system. Let's just go with a lottery like all the other schools so that any lazy fool can get the best seats in the house while us dedicated fans are stuck in the back of the stands.

I realize all of you are upperclassmen. You've been in this tent as long as I have this season. All of you have proven yourselves to be as dedicated to Krzyzewskiville as I am. Although I've probably heard every one of you complain at some point, at least you're paying your dues, while many upperclassmen decide not to. Why aren't they out here right now? Don't they realize that part of being at Duke is tenting in K-ville? Who cares that it might be a little cold, or a little inconvenient? They just need to remember that there are tons of people in the world willing to give anything to trade places with us. Who else can get into a basketball game in Cameron, let alone for free? I know when I'm a senior I'll still be here in K-ville, waiting in line as the quintessential Cameron Crazie, spending months outside.

THE ECONOMICS MAJOR

he Freshman's story caused a verbal commotion among the more senior members of his tent. Remember, too, that this Freshman was shy. He did not enjoy being at the center of the controversy he had created. Although everyone agreed that he was impressively enthusiastic about the tenting experience, further responses to the Freshman's tale varied drastically from student to student. Some tenters agreed on the laxity of the system. The Captain could be heard saying, "We probably have gotten too many graces this season."

Others scorned the Freshman's zealous condemnations. Many thought the line monitors were doing an acceptable job. "They know what they're doing this year," argued the Public Policy Major. "We have to spend time in the tents, but we've also had time to take part in activities outside of K-ville."

Still others believed that the line monitors should make tenting easier. "Thanks to K-ville, I've hardly had time for church," complained the Pre-Law Student.

"If not for God, you've certainly made time for boys," joked the Women's Studies Major, a remark that inspired a fit of bickering that I dare not relate here.

Most every topic of tenting concern came into dispute, from the required time in line to the complacency of the fans. There were even some comments about the pitiful enthusiasm of this year's freshmen. But the voice which sounded above the rest came from the Economics Major, so here follows her words.

"Although there is some truth to your observations," she said as she looked down her nose at the Freshman, "I know from experience that a true fan should not have to prove his or her dedication outside the actual games by huddling in the cold. Take me, for example. I love Duke basketball. In truth, I love all things Duke. I've been a fan my entire life, because I was raised hearing stories about this school. I'm a third generation Dukie. Can anyone else here say the same? My earliest memories include watching Duke athletics on my father's knee. I grew up planning to attend school in Durham, and I've been visiting this campus with my grandfather since I first started walking. Although my memories of Duke sporting events are some of my favorite memories from my childhood, I would probably be the first person to opt not to tent if given the opportunity of hassle-free tickets."

An astonished gasp from many members of the tent followed the Economics Major's revelation. Personally, I had considered her one of Duke basketball's most dedicated fans. She perhaps has more knowledge of the program's history than any other student at this school. Knowing her passion for the university,

I admit my surprise to discover her dislike of tenting. After her disclosure, the Economics Major allowed for a brief pause in the conversation in order to let her words sink in better. Her eyes traversed our questioning expressions while the rain made soft ripples in the fabric of the tent. But the Economics Major did not keep her listeners in suspense too long. She explained, "I would opt not to tent if I had the choice simply because tenting is a means to an end. I'm here to see a basketball game, not wait in line. Fanatical students like you force me outside." At this point her attention swung once again to the Freshman, whose face had grown pale beneath his curly red hair. "Because of you," she continued, "and people with your mentality, I can't simply go to a game and enjoy Duke basketball. I don't spend days and nights awaiting Duke football games. I've never once had a problem seeing a Duke baseball game. I'm not even forced to wait outside Cameron forever to see those games played by our incredible women's basketball program. But men's basketball, my favorite of all, I can't see without temporarily moving out of my residence hall. Every year I move away from a well-furnished room and the conveniences of indoor plumbing only to find myself living in a paper-thin shelter during the coldest months of the year!

"The fact that I'm not a fan of waiting in line for large chunks of my life has no bearing on my dedication to Duke basketball. I challenge anyone here to prove otherwise. However, although all games equally deserve our attendance, I recognize that more students want to attend the supposedly more important games. Therefore, I accept that I, in order to get the best seats, must sacrifice more time. But I still think almost anyone will agree that spending two months in Krzyzewskiville far surpasses any reasonable requirements. I should be able to love basketball and still take part in other activities on campus. But sometimes it seems that I can't because of people like this Freshman. You don't deserve to be called a Cameron Crazie. You're not concerned with the basketball. You're a Camping Crazie: all you care about is waiting in line.

"Why do you complain about dedication? Who cares if everyone spends one less night in their tents? How does not wanting to be cold, or wanting to do my homework, affect my dedication to the team? And allow me a quick word about this 'integrity of the line' phrase I'm always hearing. Explain to me how less tenting diminishes the line's purpose. The line's 'integrity' should only apply to the order being disrupted through dishonest events such as the case back in 1998. Integrity should not be a word assigned to grace periods!"

A minute or two of silence passed among the tenters at the end of the Economics Major's unexpected lecture. But, as is always the case with silence, it eventually ended. As usual, it was the words of our Host that intruded on the quiet. "Well, I see you have a strong opinion as to whether or not K-ville is necessary. As an outsider to this tenting tradition, I honestly can't see the purpose of all the extra waiting in line either. One or two nights was sufficient back in my day as a student here, and we were still plenty enthusiastic once inside the stadium. But now I've interrupted our game with my own musings. Dare I ask if this lifetime fan cares to elaborate on her tenting opinions with a story? You see, we must get back to our game. You'll be happy to recall that tenting for this basketball game has nearly ended; however, we must finish our stories before that happens. What say you? Shall we hear more?"

"Actually," came her reply, "I've got the perfect story for all of you, and I think it will better explain my view. First, allow me to add a word or two to my previous remarks. I must clarify that I don't dislike K-ville. I've had plenty of enjoyable moments out here, too. The excessive time troubles me most, and not the existence of Krzyzewskiville itself.

"From the perspective of an economist, K-ville constitutes a classic example of the *prisoner's dilemma*. You see, when students . . ."

"*Prisoner's dilemma?*" interrupted the Host as he stopped writing and looked up from his notepad. "What's that?"

"Sorry," answered our Economics Major, "I forgot that not everyone in this tent has taken the same classes I have. Allow me to explain. In social science theory, there is a famous model: that of the prisoner's dilemma. When two people are accused of having committed a crime together, the judicial system can choose to keep the suspects separate and inhibit any communication. Soon, each prisoner is approached individually and offered a deal if he will testify against his criminal partner. The prisoner, knowing only that his cohort was likely offered the same deal, has to make a decision about how to act. He can either deny the charge or confess. If he denies the charge and his partner does the same, the two prisoners have left the district attorney with a weakened case against the two accused, giving both men a better chance at acquittal, or at least a lesser sentence. If he denies the charge and his partner confesses to the court, that results in a harsher sentence for him and a much lighter sentence for the person who confessed up front. If, on the other hand, he confesses, and his partner does not, he leaves the partner high and dry, while he himself receives the lesser sentence. Or else he confesses in the hopes of helping himself, but his partner confesses as well, thus negating the chance of a lessened sentence for both men and giving the prosecutors all of their desired evidence. Thus, the prisoner has the dilemma of choosing his response based on what he thinks his partner in crime will do."

"And how does that relate to tenting?" asked our game's Host, without looking up from the notes he had resumed taking.

"I was just about to get to that," answered the Economics Major. She cleared her throat and straightened her back as she prepared to answer. It looked as if she were about to unveil a new piece of theory at an economists' convention. "In terms of K-ville, a very similar dilemma holds true with regard to when and how students choose to pitch their tents. On one hand, if a group chooses to bide its time before setting up camp, and so too do all the others, then the amount of time required for camping in K-ville could be greatly diminished. If, however, a tent makes the decision to wait, but another tent doesn't, many other tents will hurry to follow the initial one, potentially placing the tent that chose to wait much farther back in line. If our hypothetical tent decides to go ahead and pitch a tent extremely early in order to guarantee a top spot in line, and no other tents appear for many days thereafter, the first tent accomplished its goal, but also had to spend wasted time waiting in line. And lastly, imagine that the sample tent chooses to start extremely early, which quickly triggers a reaction from the other students who worry about their place in line, and very soon, dozens of tents are standing in K-ville months before a game. If this is the case, then everyone loses because all of the tents have had to make a greater time commitment."

The Host scribbled a few more words, then looked to the Economics Major and said, "By all accounts, the students at this school are supposed to be fairly intelligent, right? If you presented this argument to them would they not recognize the foolishness of their own actions? Wouldn't they realize that the entire school would be better served by everyone agreeing to wait to pitch their tents?"

"You would think so," said the Economics Major with a disapproving sigh. "According to all logic, if people wanted to spend less time in order to get tickets, they could, so there must be a better reason for the existence of K-ville than insanity among the students. After all, I might sit here and complain, but then again, if I had to be out here twice as long, my decision wouldn't change."

At this point, the Economics Major went silent. When she had begun her explanation of the *tenter's dilemma*, she had looked as if her story would be immediately underway. But now she seemed to have lost her momentum entirely. I have no doubt that the other tenters noticed her hesitation as well. The silence was broken only by the rain tapping on the top of the tent. We waited. At last, the Economics Major resumed her explanation. "I suppose," she said with a plaintive tone in her voice, "that from the outside looking in, all people can see is Duke University, a school for 'smart kids'—well, that's how I've heard people refer to it. But here we are spending weeks, even months, outside in vicious weather, and for what?—two hours of basketball. But it's really not just basketball is it? It's Duke basketball. And it's really not just waiting in line. We're being part of a community with the same goal and the same love. Out here, no one cares about your race, creed, or gender. Granted, that might be because we're all too cold to care, but I imagine it has more to do with common interests we all share. We're all Duke students, and tenters, and Cameron Crazies, and we help to create a unique college group experience. What in the world would make us want to trade that?

"This evening, I had intended to tell a story of excessive waiting. I've since been searching my memories for an instance when the waiting wasn't worthwhile. And now, I get my chance to tell that story, but I can't think of a true tale with such an ending. Even a game we lost was still worth the wait. Instead, I find myself preparing to tell you the tale of when K-ville had its earliest beginning. This is the story of the impromptu Krzyzewskiville in the summer of 2004."

Although not more than ten minutes had passed since Alex had last checked the latest sports news online, some unknown force — perhaps a basketball-related sixth sense — triggered him to reopen his browser window to the sports headlines. The top story, updated since his last viewing, read "Coach K in serious discussions with L.A. Lakers."

"No way," muttered Alex while he clicked on the link to read the full story. "Maybe they're talking about a different Coach K."

Of course, Alex knew there could be no other Coach K to which the article would refer. The fact was that the Los Angeles Lakers were in the market for a new head coach, a head coach with a well-known name and a penchant for winning, and Duke University's own Mike Krzyzewski — Coach K to most of his admirers and rivals — fit the description.

The article announced a press conference to be held at Duke at 5:00 that July afternoon to discuss the potential departure of Coach K to L.A. "This can't be good," thought Alex. "Duke doesn't just call press conferences for no reason. He must be leaving."

Alex ran out of his apartment. His first stop was a nearby picnic area where a campus barbeque was being held for students attending summer classes. "I've got to tell people," he said to himself as he jogged toward the pavilion. "Maybe I can get a group of kids together to go over to the press conference. If enough of us are there, maybe we can convince him to stay."

But basketball-related news travels fast at Duke. Coach K's potential departure couldn't have been mentioned more than fifteen minutes earlier, and yet, by the time Alex had reached the picnic area, discussion of the defection was all that could be heard among the thirty-odd people at the barbeque. Alex recognized one of his tent mates from the previous basketball season sitting at a nearby table, a fellow basketball-lover by the name of Rob. Alex sat down next to his friend and, without a word about the topic, said, "What are we going to do?"

"I have no idea," answered Rob, knowing exactly to what Alex referred. "What can we do?"

The two students sat next to each other without talking, or even looking at one another. Instead, they listened in on the conversations surrounding them.

"I can't believe he's going to leave us," sighed a girl at an adjacent table.

"He's not going anywhere," answered the boy next to her. "He loves Duke too much. He's too important a part of the Duke community."

"I bet they're offering him a ton of money," said a boy sitting at another nearby table.

"There's no way he could want to coach at the professional

level," argued yet another of the many concerned students. "He won't be able to have total control over his team like he does here. And he won't be in charge of the athletes—they'll be in charge of him."

Alex and Rob listened to these comments, and the many others of shock, denial, and sadness inevitably associated with the unexpected news. At last, Alex spoke to his friend once more. "There must be something we can do," he said.

"Like what?" asked Rob.

"I don't know," conceded Alex, "but we shouldn't just sit here and let them take our coach from us. We've got to put up some sort of fight for him."

"But what can we do, Alex? It's the summer. There aren't enough students here to do anything major. If this were the school year, half the student body would be on their way to the press conference right now. But as it stands, all we have are these thirty people in this pavilion."

"Well, I'm at least going to head over to the stadium and the media room. If nothing else, maybe I can get a glimpse of what Coach K has to say at the press conference."

"I'm going with you," said Rob, and with those words, the two boys abandoned the free food (an impressive sacrifice for a couple of college kids), and drove over to Cameron.

News had traveled fast outside the Duke community as well. Three television vans were lined up on the sidewalk, and two more were entering the closest parking lot as Alex and Rob approached the stadium. They walked into the student entrance, as they had done many times before, but never with the same sense of foreboding that they felt now.

The K-ville lawn outside the stadium was empty: a horde of students had not, after all, turned out to show their support. Inside the stadium, Alex attempted to enter the media room where the press conference would be held, but security wouldn't let him past the door. "I'm a student. I have as much of a right to be here as anyone else," he reasoned, but with no luck. He would not be admitted into the conference. Instead, Alex sat down next to Rob on the floor outside the media room. They, and a few other concerned onlookers, were staring into a small black-and-white television monitor displaying a live feed of the events next door. Joe Alleva, Duke's athletics director, took the stage behind a panel of microphones to announce the dreaded news.

"I'm here today," Alleva said, with a firm but slightly quivering voice, "to confirm that Coach Krzyzewski is currently in serious discussions with the Los Angeles Lakers about filling their head coaching vacancy."

"So that was the news?" said a disbelieving Rob. "He's announcing what we already know?"

"What does 'serious discussions' mean?" asked Alex. "Is he or isn't he staying to coach at Duke?"

The press conference clarified almost nothing. When asked to elaborate, Alleva could say little more about the situation. When asked Duke's stance, he stated the obvious. "We're going to do everything we can to make sure Coach K stays at Duke," said the athletics director, as if anyone in the room, or indeed in the country, thought the school would welcome the departure of its beloved icon.

"Well, I'm at least a bit relieved," said Rob as the two friends left the stadium. "I thought he was already on his way out, and that's why they called the press conference. Now there's still the chance that he'll stay."

"But they said the talks are serious," said Alex. "We just lost two of our top players for next year to the NBA draft, so now seems like the perfect time to duck out of this job before what looks like a tough season."

"Do you really think that Coach K would abandon us like that?" asked Rob.

"I don't think he'd abandon us. I'm just wondering if he might be thinking that now would be a good time to move on. Let's be realistic. It might be a down year. On top of that, he's been offered a chance to coach the Lakers, one of the premier programs in the history of basketball. We couldn't really blame him if he does decide to leave. At least, I wouldn't."

Alex and Rob stood on the lawn outside of Cameron, Coach K's office looming portentously in the tower behind them. Next to the boys was the blue and white sign labeling the lawn *Krzyzewskiville*. Rob looked over at the sign, shook his head, and said, "This place won't mean much without Krzyzewski."

After staring at the sign in silence with Rob, Alex said, "Well, if we're going to lose Coach K, I'm not letting him go without one last K-ville. I'm going to set up Tent 1."

"Tent 1 for what?" asked Rob. "Not the Carolina game next year?"

"No," said Alex with a smile, "I'm going to set up Tent 1 to be the first in line for Coach K's press conference announcing that he's staying at Duke. And you and I are going to get everyone we can to come out here with us. Rob, my boy, K-ville's going up a little early this year."

"You're damn right it is!"

The rest of the afternoon was spent gathering people to come out to K-ville to show Coach K how much he means to both the school and the community. Rob sent out e-mails, called anyone he knew to be in or near Durham, and began stopping people on the main quad and telling them to come out to K-ville that night.

Meanwhile, Alex had two important tasks of his own. His first job was to contact the local and national news outlets. "If we're going to be out there tonight," he thought, "then we're going to make sure that Coach K sees us." His second job was to get a tent. After all, it was the summer, and he hadn't been planning on tenting in K-ville for at least six months.

And so, Krzyzewskiville made an unusual appearance in the summer of 2004. Few students were at school, and indeed, basketball season was months away. Instead of the thousand kids inhabiting K-ville during the school year, capacity during the summer tenting season might have peaked around two hundred. Included in that number was none other than the new president of the university, Dr. Richard Brodhead. As fate would have it, the very day that brought news of Coach K's possible departure was also the day that President Brodhead took his office. And he, along with all those who found their way to that makeshift Krzyzewskiville, sent their message as loud and clear as possible. They sang their cheers of "Coach K, please stay!" long into the night. And in the end, after a weekend of discussion, stressful anticipation, and curiosity-filled nights, the decision was revealed. Coach K would stay.

HERE FOLLOWS AN EPILOGUE
TO THE ECONOMICS MAJOR'S TALE

"I think Coach K's response to the Lakers job explains what brings students out to K-ville, year after year. In the face of the offer of an extremely lucrative contract and a chance to coach a celebrated franchise, Coach K elected not to accept the invitation to L.A. And the reason why: he couldn't leave Duke. He couldn't leave this school, these students, and this community. Sometimes the intangibles are more significant than the material benefits. And that's the case with Krzyzewskiville. On the surface, the sacrifices the system requires appear to outweigh the benefits. But once you've done it, whether or not you choose to tent again, you'll likely have no regrets. The intangibles — the energy, the camaraderie, the spirit of K-ville and love of the Duke team — make tenting a singular experience, one that is worth every second of sacrifice."

With these words, the Economics Major finished her tale of Krzyzewskiville and offered another reason to our guest as to why we tent. All her companions agreed with her explanation and applauded her story, but the Host would not settle for *intangibles* as an authoritative reason for tenting. "It's great that you love your school," replied our Host. "But let's not forget that I went here too, and yet, my friends and I didn't spend two months in line waiting for basketball games. One thing you do have that we did not, however, is Coach Krzyzewski. So tell me, if Coach K had left, would that have been the end of K-ville?

"Certainly not!" cried the Freshman, abruptly.

"And how do you know that?" asked the journalist.

The nervous Freshman paused, searching for a proper response. His older brother, our Captain, came to his rescue by saying, "Of course Krzyzewskiville won't end if Coach K leaves. Or, I should say, if it does, then this is not the wonderful tradition we claim it to be. What you have to understand, and what everyone has to remember, is that Krzyzewskiville and Duke basketball are about more than one coach and his team. Yes, Coach K is a vital piece of Duke's past and present. But this school, this program, and this tent city do not depend on him. Coach K is not one of our classmates. He's not a fellow student. When we support the team, we're cheering for the coach and the players. When Coach K does leave, as he inevitably will, we can't stop supporting the players or the school.

"As for Krzyzewskiville: it might bear Coach K's name, but so too was Cameron Indoor Stadium named for a Duke athletics legend. The building was named to honor Eddie Cameron for what he had already done for the school, not on the condition of his continued support. Krzyzewskiville will always be Krzyzewskiville, with or without Coach K. We've given this tent city its title not to hold Coach K as a hostage to the school, but to honor him for the services he has already given."

When the Economics Major had finished her musings about K-ville and the Captain had completed his addition, everyone in the tent remained silent (except for the Engineer, who could still be heard snoring). If others in the tent had similar thoughts to my own, they were likely reflecting on their past experiences in this tent village. But while we within the tent were immersed in self-reflection, voices began to grow louder in the rest of K-ville.

"Why are there so many people moving around outside?" asked the Pre-Med Student.

"I don't know," answered the Math Major. "Do you think the line monitors are coming? Maybe they're about to call a check."

"This can't be!" cried the Host. "We're only halfway through our contest. If we end now, this storytelling competition will remain unfinished. And what good could come of a competition with no ending?"

The Captain shook his head from side to side and said, "It's only eleven o'clock. There's no way that they would call a check this early. They want us to earn our spots in the game."

"But it is raining," reminded the Women's Studies Major.

"Maybe they've decided that there's no point in keeping so many of us out here in the bad weather."

I think I heard the Freshman mumble the words "I hope not," but no one else in the tent heard. Or, if they did, they took no notice.

"And because of the rain," said the Pre-Law Student, "people wouldn't be outside for any other reason than a check."

"I'll go see what's happening," I suggested.

The Pre-Med Student replied, "You can borrow my umbrella." The umbrella, I remembered, was pink.

"That's okay," I said. "I don't think it's raining too hard, and I'll only be outside for a minute." I tied my shoes, buttoned my coat, and stuffed my hands into my pockets. I lingered under the shelter of the tent's overhang for a few more seconds, took a deep breath, and then stepped into the cold, January downpour.

The noise was coming from the direction of Cameron, so I headed toward the student entrance. Underneath the overhanging archways outside the stadium doors, a cluster of students had formed a semicircle around a central figure. I squeezed into the crowd to keep from standing in the rain, and then I whispered to the tall boy standing on my right, "What's going on?"

"Shhh!" he chided, and pointed toward the door. "Coach K is about to say something."

Sure enough, standing in the stone doorframe was none other than the revered patriarch of Duke basketball. The light from inside the stadium met the darkness of night at the threshold where he stood. The intersection of light and dark formed a yellow glow around Coach K. The black warm-up suit he wore had the word *Duke* emblazoned on the jacket. Every time he moved his arms, I could hear the distinctive *whoosh* of nylon against nylon.

"I know it's late," he began, "and I've already told my team to go home and get a good night's sleep. I hate that you guys are out here this late, especially in this rain. It's just as important for the 'sixth man' to be well rested before a game." His suggestion met with scattered applause and laughter, but he motioned us to quiet down before he would continue. "But I just want to say thank you, to all of you. I know the weather is pretty crappy, and it's a school night, and you've got other things you could be doing. But I want you to know that we really appreciate what you're all doing for us out here.

"You know, I can't tell you how proud I am to have this city named after me. The administration and the athletic department guys keep coming to me and talking about naming a building in my honor, or something like that. But I keep trying to tell them I don't need it. Why would I want a building with my name on it? Buildings are sterile objects. They don't grow, they only decay. And fifty years from now, who knows? They might come along and tear it down. They might even try to replace it with something bigger and better, and let's be honest, nobody wants to be replaced. But having a city take your name, now that's something to be proud of. You kids have created a living, growing thing. Nothing bigger and better is going to come along and replace this city, because that's the advantage of something that's alive—it can adapt to changing needs. So maybe ten years from now, this tenting thing will have grown, and it will take four months instead of, what is it now, two? God, I can't believe you kids do that. Or maybe the camping thing shrinks down to one night, or completely ends. But whether it expands or shrinks, the city is adapting to what the current atmosphere requires. In that way, K-ville can never grow old, and it can never become out of date, which means you kids have given me an honor that having ten buildings with my name on them couldn't duplicate."

The small crowd cheered for Coach K and his remarks. He pumped his fist into the air and shouted over the noise, "Now let's get ready to beat Carolina!" The cheers followed our Coach as he turned back into the building. The doors to Cameron closed, and just like that, the interruption was over.

I went back to my tent, slipped off my shoes, and unzipped the flap. Before I had both feet into the shelter, I was bombarded with questions. "What was it?" they asked. "It couldn't have been a check, right?"

I wiped the dripping hair off of my brow, shook my head and said, "No, it was just some kids gathering around outside the doors of Cameron." My peers muttered their disappointment while I squeezed once more into my seat.

AARON

ur Host must have thought that our conversation about the false check excitement had continued too long. At last he broke in and said, "Well that was far too close. We almost had to cut our game short. But who knows, the next rumble in K-ville could be a forewarning of a real personal check." No sooner had the Host spoken his words than a loud clap of thunder rumbled overhead. "Or perhaps," he suggested, "we'll have a few more rumbles before the tent check."

"They're not going to call a check during a thunderstorm," groaned the Sociology Major. "This means we'll have to be out here even longer."

"Let's not worry about that," said the Host. "We've had no trouble passing the time with our stories up to this point. Let's continue where we left off." Our Host then looked toward me and said, "What kind of tenter are you? You look as if you're searching for a lost contact. I've seen you do nothing but stare at the ground the entire night except for those few moments when you stepped outside. Come on, raise your eyes and look at all of us. Now watch out everyone. Give this man some room! He's obviously a person who enjoys the pleasures of life. His waist-line is nearly as large as mine! I bet he'd make a fine husband to any searching woman. But I would guess from his face that he's constantly causing trouble—even though he hasn't said much to us here this evening. Go ahead and tell us something, since it's now your turn. Give us a good story about Krzyzewskiville!"

"Well," I said, "just don't be disappointed, because I only know a tale in rhyme that I heard a long time ago."

"That sounds good," replied the Host. "Now, I'll bet we hear our best story, judging by the looks of this quiet tenter."

HERE BEGINS AARON'S

TALE OF RICHARD

Once there was a tenter who really loved basketball,
And he chose Duke University, with hopes of seeing all
The games played in Cameron Indoor Stadium,
And cheering on the Blue Devils in their title runs.

His name was Richard Lunstrom, hailing from Kentucky,
Where everyone considered the name Duke to be unlucky.
The reason for the animosity coming from that state
Had something do with a game played in the Elite Eight.

The year was 1992, and the place was Philadelphia.
It was Duke versus Kentucky in the city of brotherly love.
The Devils were looking to defend their first national title,
The resulting game would soon become incredible.

Matching point for point, the teams were virtually even,
And it was obvious that neither group would give in.
Ultimately they were forced into a period of overtime
Which proved each team to still be nearly equal in kind.

The score stood still at 102–103 in Kentucky's favor,
As did the clock at 2 seconds, which Duke would savor.
The three-quarter court pass left Grant Hill's hands,
And found Christian Laettner in the air. When he lands

He takes one dribble, and fakes to his right,
Then he turns left and puts the ball into flight.
From seventeen feet and double coverage,
Christian Laettner makes the improbable bucket.

The Blue Devils won, and the rest is history.
A repeat national championship ends my story
Of one of the greatest games ever played
In the long basketball history of the NCAA.

Since you now know Kentucky's hatred for the Blue Devils,
I'll return to Richard's years and experiences in many
　　K-villes . . .

HERE THE HOST INTERRUPTS
AARON'S TALE OF RICHARD

"For the love of God, please, no more," said our Host. "May
the cold freeze my eardrums before I hear another word of this

tale. To hell with this rhyming! It must be some kind of literary torture."

"Why do you say that?" I asked. "Why have you stopped me in the middle of my story, but haven't done so to anyone else? This is the best tale I know."

"To be honest," he said, "because your pitiful rhyming is getting on my nerves! And it's wasting what little time we have left. From now on, you're not allowed to rhyme. Let's see if you can tell something historical about K-ville—with any luck, in prose—and maybe you can actually teach us something we don't know about Duke basketball. After all, find me one person here who hasn't seen that famous shot! As for me, I was actually at the game."

"Gladly," I replied. "For your sake I'll tell a little story in prose which, I hope, will make you happy. If not, you're just far too picky. I'll give it plot, and history, and perhaps even some moral value just to spice it up. But bear in mind that you may have heard this tale before, although in different words. For our biggest challenge in telling tales of Krzyzewskiville is that, as you know, almost everything known about it has been broadcast by word-of-mouth, with very little written down. It's possible to hear the same story twice, and some of the events may have changed the second time around. But don't worry: a different version may reveal new subtleties. So sit back and enjoy the history I'll give to you, and please, this time, see the entire story through.

An excited wave of whispers ripples through the 1,200 residents of Krzyzewskiville. Julius cracks his eyelids. A blurred image of the gray underside of the canvas tent comes gradually into focus. As it does, Julius, exhausted, is once again aware of the numbness in the tips of his fingers. The mucus trickling from his weather-reddened nose tickles the edge of his upper lip. He tries to raise his hand to wipe away the moisture, but discovers that his arm is still trapped in the navy-blue sleeping bag. Julius takes a deep breath through his nose, hoping to relieve the itch on the tip of his upper lip. Success! The itch has subsided. He rolls onto his side and curls his knees into his chest as he tries to decipher the significance behind the loud voices around his tent.

"They're coming," he hears someone yell across the lawn. "Hurry up. You better run. They'll start any minute."

While he is still trying to make sense of the message, Julius's cell phone rings shrilly. He digs his hands through the many pockets in his jacket and finds his phone. "Now how do I get this thing to my ear?" he mutters, cocooned in the sleeping bag. Julius hastily frees his arms from the sleeping bag amid a chorus of ripping seams.

"Yo, where are you?" questions a familiar voice through the phone. "They're calling the first personal check. Are you coming out here?"

"What are you talking about?" replies Julius, "I'm lying in the tent."

"Oh," responds his friend. "Really?"

"Yes. Why would I lie about that?" asks a confused Julius.

"I just hadn't seen you out here tonight," explains his friend, sounding still unconvinced. "Well, come on out and find us so you can get your first check."

"Okay, I'm coming, just give me a second. Where can I find you?

"Meet us by the K-ville sign."

"Be right there," says Julius, and he flips the phone closed with a snap. The digital clock on the cover displays the time. "3:32 in the morning?" groans Julius. He sighs and then complains aloud as though someone is nearby to agree, "About damn time for them to call a check. So much for getting back to the room early tonight to get some studying done."

While the whispers around the tent crescendo into a cacophony of voices and footsteps, Julius unzips the sleeping bag and wriggles out from beneath the covers. Too tall to stand upright in the tent, Julius walks to the door hunched over. He pauses to rewrap the cashmere scarf around his neck and fasten the buttons on his thick wool coat. He unzips the nylon flap and steps out onto the cement walkway.

Julius's boots still sit next to the door. When he pushes his feet into the shoes, his toes sting on contact with the ice-cold leather. "I shouldn't have kept these outside," he mumbles as his fingers fumble with the laces. Julius has not yet noticed that around him, K-ville has drifted into silence.

While pulling a pair of gloves over his fingers, Julius's eyes wander around the deserted tent village. He begins to wonder whether he is alone in his end of K-ville. He can hear what sound like faint voices in the direction of Cameron. However, a heavy silver fog clouds his vision and he can't see the stadium. Where he stands, near the IM building, all the other tenters have vanished.

"How long did it take me to get out of that sleeping bag?" Julius asks himself. "I could have sworn that I just heard voices right outside the tent. I guess I better hurry. I don't want to miss the check. I'll just cut in between the tents."

Although the fog had felt thick when Julius first stepped into the open air, it seemed to have closed even tighter around the Duke junior while he was surveying his surroundings. It is now too thick to determine the direction of the IM Building, the Wilson Rec Center, or Cameron. He only knows that his tent must still be behind him. He turns around and espies the shape of the blue and gray canvas structure. With his hands out in front of him, he feels his way around it, and enters the recesses of Krzyzewskiville through the path between his tent and his neighbor's.

Once inside the tent city, all sounds vanish. Lucky for Julius, so too does the blanket of fog. But, despite the fog having lifted, he discovers that the heart of K-ville is difficult to navigate without the aid of daylight. The tents form walls alongside of him.

Running between the multicolored canvases are seemingly identical narrow passages. "Which way do I go?" Julius wonders. He creeps forward in what he decides to be the direction of the voices he had heard earlier.

Instead of cutting straight through the center of K-ville, as Julius had planned, the tent corridors twist left, then right, and at times seem to double back on themselves. At every intersection Julius is forced to take an increasingly uneducated guess as to which direction to turn. Complicating Julius's journey is an obstacle course of ropes securing each tent. In order to pass through the maze, he has to duck under, climb over, or squeeze through the web of twine anchoring Krzyzewskiville to the earth.

But Julius continues to maneuver through the path. As he does so, he begins to notice that the number of ropes obstructing his course grow fewer and fewer. After sliding through two particularly close and taut lines, Julius steps into a circular clearing in the tents. This deep into K-ville, the orange light of the lamps along the periphery has faded to a meager glow. The clearing is illuminated by the pale reflection of the half-moon. With help from the moonlight, Julius searches for a direction to take, but discovers that there are no spaces between any of the tents surrounding him. Either there are too many ropes to pass through the gap between structures, or the tents are actually touching one another and leave no room to pass between them.

"Who pitches a tent touching his neighbors?" thinks Julius. "Has K-ville really become that popular that we've run out of space to separate tents? This place is starting to look like one of those new suburban developments where you can sneeze in your kitchen and your neighbor's so close that he can yell 'God bless you' from his bathroom. Durham must be getting too crowded. Our suburban tent city is succumbing to urban sprawl!"

Julius cannot spot an easy exit. He turns around to retrace his steps, but when he does, he discovers that his path has been sealed off by yet another tent. "What the . . ." he begins to curse, but he is interrupted by a throaty laugh. Julius pivots to see the owner of the voice. He finds himself standing face to face with a stout and burly man. His thinning silver hair is slicked back, and he sports a thin mustache that twirls towards the heavens at its tips. Under his left arm he carries a clipboard, and under his right he has tucked a black cap with a patch on the front labeling him the Durham County fire marshal.

"Is this your tent?" asks the gruff voice.

"No, sir," stutters Julius, uncertain of which tent the fire marshal is suggesting belongs to him.

"Don't lie to me!" scolds the official. "Why else would you be standing here? I don't see anyone else nearby."

"I was just . . . just . . . uh, looking for my friends, sir. I was cutting through tents to get there faster."

"Do you expect me to believe that? Do you realize that you're putting your life and the lives of all these other students in danger by running all those electrical cords to your tent?"

Julius looks over the fire marshal's shoulder toward the tent that had been mistakenly identified as his. Running into the tent are hundreds of extension cords entering from every side. "But, that's not my tent . . ." he tries to explain.

The officer interrupts Julius, saying "You aren't leaving here until you've taken down that fire hazard. When you're done with that, I'm kicking you out of K-ville for good. Don't ever expect to see another basketball game on this campus. If I could, I would have you kicked out of school!"

The surly officer reaches for Julius's arm, but Julius is too quick. He jumps back from the fire marshal and runs toward a patch of ropes between a pair of tents. Without looking back, he dives into the crisscrossed tangles and struggles through the wires, ripping his pants in the process.

The ropes thin out and eventually spread far enough apart to form a path through which Julius can navigate. He has escaped the fire marshal, and feeling confident that the man's girth would prohibit him from following the same path, Julius takes a few minutes to relax. He leans against a wooden pole which someone has anchored into the ground. Secured at its top is a miniature backboard and basketball hoop.

Julius enjoys little time to catch his breath before he spots the shadowy outline of a person approaching him from between two tents. On first sight he fears that the marshal has found another path through the city. But Julius realizes that, unlike the squat city official, the person walking toward him is imposingly tall. He cannot be the same man. Before Julius recognizes the features of the approaching figure, the small goal behind him begins to grow. Julius backs away from the post in fear, but stumbles over a rope and falls to the ground. Lying on his back, he looks up and watches as the makeshift basket magically morphs into a regulation goal. He then feels the mud beneath his hands begin to harden. He looks down and sees that what once had been earth has now transformed into the high-gloss hardwood of a basketball court.

The tall figure that had been approaching now stands next to the fallen tenter. Although he cannot see the man's face, Julius can see the hand that has been extended to help him up. He takes the gracious hand—it dwarfs his own—and is pulled to his feet. After brushing himself off, Julius looks up to say *thank you*. When he does so, he discovers the identity of the stranger. Standing before him, dressed in his white and blue basketball jersey, is Duke's (and the ACC's) record holder for most consecutive free throws made—J. J. Redick.

"What are you doing here?" Julius stutters.

Redick ignores the question and walks to the free throw line. Once there, he turns toward Julius and explains his instructions. "It's time to prove your abilities as a fan," says Redick. "If you want to pass by this court, you must first cause me to miss a free throw. You'll have five chances to distract me."

"And what happens if you don't miss?" asks Julius, not certain of what awaits him, but not wanting to return to what he has already escaped.

"The only way out is to follow the path forward. Without

passing my test, you'll never be able to leave Krzyzewskiville." Redick squares himself to the line and begins his routine. He dribbles the ball, spins it in his hands, dribbles once more, and then, in one smooth motion, he lifts the ball up and releases it into the air. It spins effortlessly through the breeze, floats into the hoop, and touches nothing but the twine of the net. "You'll have to do better than that if you want to distract me," says Redick with a smile. Julius watches as the ball magically bounces back into the shooter's hands.

When the shooter begins his routine anew, Julius, having no other ideas, starts to yell as loud as his vocal cords will allow. This tactic has no effect on Redick; once again, he releases the ball and it drops through the hoop without a noise. Julius has only three more chances.

On the next shot Julius waits for Redick to raise the ball, then he shouts "Miss it!" just as the ball leaves the shooter's hands. Through the net the ball goes, as if Redick's hand has been guiding it all the way to the rim. Two shots remain.

Unbuttoning his coat while sprinting toward the basket, Julius focuses on another idea for how to create a distraction. He pulls off his coat and stands behind the goal. He whips his jacket in circles over his head while shouting and jumping in Redick's line of sight. Without so much as a glance toward the commotion, Redick takes his fourth shot. Julius watches the ball fly. He feels as though he's watching a recording of the previous three attempts. The ball drops through the rim and bounces back into the player's hands. Julius now faces his fifth and final chance to prove his abilities as a fan.

"I don't know what else to do," Julius despairs. "I don't think I'll be able to pass this test. I guess I'm a failure as a fan." He puts his coat back on and walks out from behind the goal. Stopping midway between Redick and the hoop, and stepping outside of the lane, Julius raises his hands in the air in silent anticipation of the free throw to be made. As he had done on the four previous occasions, Redick executes a flawless shot, and the ball glides into the basket. Julius pulls his hands down while mumbling "woosh," just as he had done while watching countless free throws during games in Cameron. He then faces the shooter and applauds the perfection.

"You may pass," says Redick.

Julius's eyes widen with disbelief. "I don't understand," asks the puzzled student, "you made all five free throws."

"But the real test isn't for you to distract me," explains Redick. "Always remember that your first responsibility as a Cameron Crazie is to support our team, not disrupt the opponent." With these final words, the basketball court and the shooter fade back into darkness, and the path reappears without any obstructions.

Julius trots cautiously through the still curving maze of tents. He wants to find an exit, but he also hopes to avoid any other detours. When he comes to the end of a blind curve, the trail opens into a straightaway. However, blocking his path is a row of four gray plastic utility garbage cans. Beyond the row of four is a row of three, beyond that is a row of two, and at the tip of a triangle is a single receptacle.

Julius examines the odd obstruction in order to determine how he can pass. He looks up toward the road ahead and sees a mirror image of the ten-can triangle blocking his path approximately fifty feet ahead. Behind the distant setup looms the wide silhouette of a person frighteningly reminiscent of the fire marshal. But when the voice speaks, the pitch is higher and the tone not as scratchy. "Is that another student?" questions Julius.

"To pass," shouts the unfamiliar voice, "you must first defeat me in a game of ultimate Beirut."

As Julius hears the stranger's command, he notices a white minifridge appear to his left. "Gee . . . I wonder what could be in here." He opens the door to reveal the sight of ten cans of beer. "One for each garbage can, I assume," says Julius with a smile. "Now this is one challenge I think I can handle."

"Heads up!" yells the voice from across the way. Julius looks up in time to see a football fall into the can at the tip of his triangle. He shrugs, reaches into the fridge, and removes a beer.

"Bottom's up!" says Julius. The can hisses when he pulls the tab. He tilts his head back, and with four gulps the beer is gone. The can in which the football had fallen disappears while he chugs. At the same time, a football materializes on top of the refrigerator. Julius crushes the aluminum can and drops it onto the ground while reaching for the football with his other hand. With the laces resting comfortably in his palm, Julius takes a couple of steps forward and releases the ball. It spirals across the field and drops into a barrel. Then Julius hears a hissing sound, followed soon thereafter by a loud belch.

Back over the field arcs the football, but this time Julius catches it as it flies past the remaining nine goals. "Damn . . . no beer for me this time," he says, and he tosses the football back in the direction from which it had come. Another garbage can of his opponent's filled, another beer gone.

The score reaches five to one before Julius deflects an errant shot into one of his own cans. He hears a slurred voice argue, "Hey, that one still counts."

"Damn right it does," chimes Julius as he reaches for another beer. "Good thing, too. I'm getting thirsty."

Thanks to his experience as a quarterback in high school, Julius misses only one shot throughout the course of the game. On the other hand, his unknown opponent, because of the continued consumption of beer, gets predictably worse as the event drags on. The final score is ten to two when the remaining eight trash cans disappear from the path in front of Julius. Before he proceeds forward, he turns to the left, but discovers that when the cans disappeared so too did the minifridge. "Damn," sighs the disappointed victor. "I should have helped him with one more shot."

With his thoughts returning to the check he is bound to be missing, Julius begins to sprint through the open passageway in front of him. He leaps over the body of his passed-out Beirut opponent and follows the narrow but now straight path. As he runs, the sun begins to rise. The color patterns of the tents around him become more visible, and in the growing light Julius recognizes the shape of the blue sign labeling Krzyzewskiville. "At last," he huffs, "I'm almost there."

Julius's focus on the sign causes him to overlook the growing softness of the ground. It gets worse with every step. As his feet begin to sink, his run turns into a jog, then a walk, then a trudge until he can go no further. The sign, however, has not come any nearer. Meanwhile, Julius can no longer move his feet.

"So close, but still a ways to go," says an airy voice from behind Julius. He tries to turn his head, but his legs are too entrenched in the mud for him to fully rotate his body.

"Who are you?" asks Julius, but the voice will not answer his question.

"If you would like to go further, you must first provide me with three answers. To prove yourself a worthy Crazie, I will now test your knowledge of Duke basketball."

"What kind of knowledge?" asks Julius, stalling for time to gather his thoughts. The voice from behind him disregards the question and asks its own.

"We'll start easy," says the voice, "Having scored 2,556 points over his four-year career, this man's name and number now hang from the rafters in Cameron. Always a scorer, from his first time on the court, this person was the first and so far the only freshman to lead his Duke team in points per game. Of which former Duke great do I speak?"

"That's easy," scoffs Julius, relieved that he knows the answer to this first question. "You're describing the career of longtime associate head coach, Johnny Dawkins."

"Think it was easy, huh? Well, good for you. But here's another question; let's see how you do. Since basketball began at Duke, over one hundred years ago, some of the greatest players to take the court have worn the blue and white colors of Duke. But in that time, despite the many stars and All-Americans, only two players from Duke have ever been taken first overall in the NBA draft. The second of the two is recent and from Coach K's era, but can you name the first one?"

"You're right, that is a harder question," sighs Julius. "However," he continues, "I just read a book about Cameron the other day which gave the answer. Art Heyman was the first Blue Devil to be selected number one in the draft. If you want to stop me, you'll have to do better than that."

"You want a harder question, do you? Well here's one for you. Tell me, Julius, what is your favorite Duke basketball game?"

Knowing facts and statistics about the program is one thing, but choosing a favorite game is indeed a challenge. Julius begins recalling some of the many games he has watched both before and during his college career. The first that comes to mind is the Duke-Kentucky match-up on the way to the National Championship in 1992. "But that's not my favorite," he tells himself. "I've only seen recordings of it." Other games spring to memory. He thinks about the one against Maryland when Jason Williams scored eight of the ten points needed in the final minute to tie the game and complete one of the most impressive comebacks in basketball history. He even recalls the Duke women's team's 2004 visit to UConn where they mounted a rally from twenty points down to win on a final-second three-pointer by Jessica Foley.

"I'm sorry, but I can't answer that question," comes Julius's response. "It's impossible for me to choose one game to call my favorite. Every game I've watched I've loved because, in all honesty, I love both the program and the school it represents."

The mud in front of Julius begins to sprout grass, and the ground beneath his feet becomes solid once again. He pushes himself up from the soft earth surrounding him, struggles to his feet, and resumes his run toward the sign. But once more his pace slows as he draws closer. Another figure stands next to the sign that reads *Krzyzewskiville*. Julius hopes he has, at last, found his friend. But he realizes that the figure is too tall for it to be his acquaintance.

Julius stops within ten feet of the sign and the stranger, but all he can see is the back of a man in a black suit. "Hello," says Julius, though it is perhaps more of a question than a greeting.

"Hello, Julius," responds the stranger as he turns.

A smile flashes across Julius's face and he exclaims, "Coach K! What are you doing out here?"

"I'm here to see you, Julius. I'm your coach too," he answers as he faces the disheveled student. "After all, by tenting, haven't you proven yourself to be a worthy part of my team? And have you not just spent the entire night simply trying to get to your personal check before the game?"

"Oh . . . I was so busy trying to get out of there that I had kind of forgotten about the check. I suppose by now I've probably missed too many of them."

"I wouldn't worry about that," suggests Coach K. "Your efforts tonight have undoubtedly proven your dedication."

Julius thinks about his surroundings for a minute. He looks around, but still sees no other students. The sun no longer appears to be rising, but it does not seem to be sinking lower either. He asks his Coach, "How do you know about what's gone on tonight?"

"Did you not notice a connection between the tasks you faced? They were by no means random. Each of them was training for your part on this team."

"I don't understand. What team?"

"You're a part of this team, Julius, just like any of the players. Without our fans, the program can't be successful. All those tasks related to your responsibility as a fan. Your job is to be dedicated, supportive, and safe, and to still have fun."

"But how are the fans as important as the players? Those guys are the ones who do all the work. We just watch them."

"Duke basketball can't exist without Duke University. This program represents the school. It represents you, your classmates, the employees, and the alumni. There's no purpose in the team's existence if it's distinguished from the institution." At this point, Coach K turns to the blue sign bearing the name of the city christened in his honor. He smiles, and then continues, saying, "To you, this village, Krzyzewskiville, exists for the basketball program. Try not to forget that the reverse is also true. The basketball program represents you, and perhaps that should be your best reason for supporting it. The effort and dedication you and your fellow tenters exhibit characterize the outstanding caliber of Duke's students."

Without another word, Coach K leaves Julius standing outside Krzyzewskiville while he strides back toward Cameron. He disappears into a door, and Julius finds himself alone again. But while he walks back toward his tent, this time following the sidewalk path, Julius swears he can hear behind him the cheering of a packed stadium.

HERE FOLLOWS THE EPILOGUE
TO AARON'S TALE

When I had finished my story concerning the adventures of Julius in K-ville, the Host turned to me and said, "That was a most unexpected tale and a nice change of pace. I daresay, however, it was not very historical."

I smiled toward the Host, but did not reply. I knew that our Host understood the meaning in my tale, and I had already taken enough time with my lengthy story. Our Host, however, did not hesitate in moving us to our next speaker. "Oh my," he said, "time is running out with every minute we spend in idle conversation." His eyes scanned the crowd to see who had yet to tell a story until, at last, they focused on the Women's Studies Major. "Right now," he began, "we'll continue to move through the group. I think, since we have yet to hear from you"—he nodded toward the Women's Studies Major—"I'll ask you first. If you would, please give us the pleasure of your tale about Krzyzewskiville."

"Certainly," she said. "Hopefully it will please you—you and this wonderful company of friends."

She then, very seriously, began her tale, which now follows.

THE WOMEN'S STUDIES MAJOR

"My experience gives me sufficient right to speak of a glaring problem within the athletics program, not only at this school, but at virtually every school in the country—and, I might add, even beyond the confines of the college campus. It's hard to find women's athletics programs that receive the same respect, appreciation, and funding as do similar programs for men. The reason I raise this particular issue this evening and in this very tent is that the women's basketball program here at Duke highlights perfectly the inequalities that women athletes face today. I would hope that every student supports the women's program and its players in all of their endeavors and accomplishments. They are, after all, your fellow Duke students. However, the lack of expression of this support for our women athletes deserves attention. Even men's sports at Duke with less stature and success appear more visibly supported than our dominating women's basketball program.

"The women's basketball team has, in recent years, become one of the top programs in the country, nearly on the same level as the storied Tennessee and Connecticut teams, both of which have repeatedly been national champions. But in stark contrast to those two schools, our stadium has almost never been sold out for a women's game. Even for the annual home game against the Tar Heels, the stadium might not reach capacity. If the most famous college basketball rivalry fails to pack the house, imagine what the attendance for games against lesser opponents must be like. But here we are, the temperature is nearly below freezing, the rain is pouring down, and we're waiting in line outside to see the men's teams face off tomorrow night.

"As for myself, I haven't missed a women's home game since I've been a student at Duke. In addition, I've lived in Durham all my life, so I had the opportunity to see plenty of games as I grew up. Since the men's basketball games are always packed, the women's team draws a following from the Durham-area Duke fans who can't find or afford tickets to the more prominent program's games. But once you see the women play, it's hard to deny that they're not just as skilled as the men. I can remember back when Coach Goestenkors first got here for the 1992–93 season. Let's just say that at that time, there was probably good reason for poor turnout at the women's games. The men were coming off their second straight national championship, and here was Coach G's team with a 12–15 record—3–13 in the ACC. It's no wonder her program was getting overlooked. But since then she hasn't had a losing season, and the Duke name has slowly moved to the top of the women's national rankings. The team has seen three NCAA Final Fours and made a host of other appearances in the national tournament during Coach G's tenure. The Duke women's program was the first to go undefeated (19-0) in the ACC schedule, including ACC tournament play, and then to do it twice—in succession. Let's see the men's team do that. With these impressive accomplishments, I can't imagine why anyone would not want to come out and see the women play.

"I've heard all the excuses why students don't show up for women's games, but none of them are really acceptable. The excuse I hear the most is that other schools are bigger. Students complain that UConn and Tennessee have larger fan bases than Duke because they're significantly larger universities. People try to convince me that they have more students and more alumni to draw support from for every game. They complain that students don't have the extra time to always go out for games to support both the men's and women's basketball teams, and that it's too much of a time commitment with tenting and classes. Well, I'll grant you that other schools are larger, but I counter that we have fewer seats to fill because Cameron Indoor Stadium is smaller. But more important is the fact that supporting women's basketball doesn't require the same kind of time commitment as does supporting our men's basketball program. You have to be in line at least two hours before a game to see the men play, but you can walk right into a women's game and find incredible seats.

"Using tenting for men's games as an excuse not to attend women's games is also pitiful. First of all, the population of K-ville will reach at most around 1,300 students. Since the undergraduate population is around 6,500, and there are hundreds more graduate- and professional-school students on top of that, obviously not everyone is precluded from attending women's games because of their tenting duties. And, of course, we all know very well that graces are given to tenters who want to watch the women's team play—so, if you *do* happen to have a shift during a women's game, there's no reason you can't catch some great women's basketball instead. After all, if you're bothering to tent in the first place, doesn't that make you a dedicated basketball fan? And because you're such a fan of basketball, is it not logical for you to want to watch every game possible?

"Another excuse I've often heard is that our women's team doesn't have any stiff competition since the level of most opposing women's programs is not of the same caliber as the same schools' men's programs. People claim that the Duke women are always going to win, and at this excuse, I just have to laugh! Since when did a team's consistent winning become a deterrent to watching them play? It seems to me that losing is what should turn people away. Have we at Duke become so spoiled with our basketball that we apparently can't even be happy about being successful? Have you ever heard a more ridiculous reason not to support an athletics program than 'We're too good . . . I don't want to watch us always win'?

"And the excuse that probably grates on me the most is when people complain that the women's games aren't as exciting as the men's. Something about less athleticism, or a slower pace, or some other pitiful reason. Women athletes are less athletic? Are you kidding me? Is that how you would describe someone like Alana Beard? She's the leading scorer, man or woman, in

Duke basketball history. Her jersey number now hangs from the rafters of Cameron. As for playing at a slower pace, I can remember countless men's games that have dragged on forever. One of the Crazies' favorite cheers is to mimic the actions of the other teams by saying *boink* with each dribble, *pass* with each pass, and *shoot* when they take a shot. That cheer was created during a game against Carolina before the shot clock was created. The overmatched Tar Heels were trying to slow the game by holding the ball; the impatient Crazies began mimicking UNC's actions to speed them up. My point is that the very existence of this cheer proves that men don't always play at a faster pace.

"Now, I can spend all night listing the many reasons we should go out to support women's basketball games, but I hope instead that my story will convince you. Take it from me, women's basketball games are just as exciting as the men's games. Once I've told my story about a specific game in our women's basketball history you'll surely agree that the excuses students fabricate for only attending men's games are sorely lacking.

BEHOLD THE WORDS
BETWEEN THE PRE-MED STUDENT
AND THE MATH MAJOR

The Math Major laughed when he had heard these words of the Women's Studies Major. "By God, as I hope for a front row seat in Cameron, that was a long preamble to a tale about equality for women! I don't recall a man's story tonight that wasted as much time in its introduction."

When the Pre-Med Student heard the Math Major's exclamation she said, "We shouldn't have expected anything less. Men are always chauvinists! See, my friends, a guy will always become defensive when trying to discuss equality for women. Why do you speak of lengthy preambles? What's the difference —amble or trot, or shut up, or leave the tent! You're interrupting our enjoyment!"

"Oh, is that it?" said the Math Major, "Now I'm sexist and a chauvinist for trying to hurry up the story. Just wait until my turn comes about. Maybe I'll tell a story about Pre-Med kids who can't handle their workloads and have to drop out."

"Feel free to do so," replied the Pre-Med Student, "and before the night is over I may tell the tale of a student majoring in math because he couldn't succeed in engineering. Or would that hit a little too close to home for your comfort?"

"Peace!" our Host cried, "and right now! Let the woman tell her story. Go ahead, my good lady, tell your tale."

"All right," replied the Women's Studies Major. "Just as you wish—as long as I have the permission of this worthy Math Major."

"Yes, of course," the Math Major said. "Tell away."

On February 1, 2003, the defending national champion, the University of Connecticut Huskies, came to town for a highly anticipated match with our Blue Devils women's team in Cameron Indoor Stadium. Both teams went into the game with a lot to prove. Not only was UCONN defending its national championship, but it was also touting a fifty-eight-game winning streak, a record in women's collegiate basketball, and a national ranking of no. 2. The Duke team was holding on to its first no. 1 ranking in the program's history, and the women had proved themselves worthy of the honor on multiple occasions, including an early-season romp over then second-ranked Tennessee. However, the Duke program was not considered on par with other elite teams, specifically because the Duke women couldn't yet claim a national championship. Defeating the Huskies would be an important test of its skill, as well as a help in validating the program.

Duke was the favorite going into the game, not only because of its higher ranking but also because of its home-court advantage. The Blue Devils could count on a rowdy turnout of Cameron Crazies to intimidate the visiting opponents. The prediction was that UCONN's streak would end in front of a sellout crowd in Cameron and a television audience from coast to coast. Sadly, only half of this prediction came true: the stadium was full, with 9,314 fans in attendance, but the majority of them left the game disappointed. That, however, is just the summary of events as it will be read years hence. But those who were there know that more happened in that game than can be conveyed by the score and statistics. With any luck, the experience redefined the relationship between Duke students and their women's basketball program.

Geno Auriemma, the UCONN coach, is known for his crass personality and controversial comments — attributes that were all the more apparent in the weeks leading up to the game. When asked how he thought the Cameron Crazies would affect his team's performance, he described the Crazies' antics as "overrated" and implied that they in no way would affect the outcome of the game. He reasoned that his program was accustomed to playing before a large audience. That logic can't be denied: his team's games consistently sold out, and the Duke women at that point had yet to see their stadium filled. But the Crazies don't take kindly to criticism. When called "overrated," they became determined to prove Auriemma wrong. They showed up en masse, tenting for the first time for a Duke women's basketball game. K-ville had already been in place for more than a month by the time of the Connecticut game. In honor of that game, however, K-ville became G-ville — named after Coach Goestenkors, of course — even if only for a few days, as students began waiting in line for the best seats to the upcoming women's game. Coach Auriemma even graced the tent city with his presence; I've seen pictures of him posing with a group of Crazies outside the tents.

Admission to women's games was handled in a different manner than admission to the men's games. Since the women's attendance base stretched much farther into Durham, patrons had already bought tickets for the traditional student section in Cameron. As a result, students could only sit on the TV side, which drastically limited the number of tenting Crazies who could be admitted. Not only was this the first women's game to be sold out, but a few hundred fans had to be turned away. In addition, both schools' prominence helped set new television rating records for a regular season women's basketball game.

Despite the somewhat decreased student accommodations, the Crazies would prove that they deserved their formidable reputation. From the moment UCONN's team stepped onto the floor, the fans made their presence known. Chants of "Husky Women" rang through the stadium, as did traditional cheers encouraging the Duke women. Coach Auriemma probably received the worst of it, being constantly taunted by his given name, which he is known to loathe: *Luigi*. In addition, students waved Australian flags in honor of Duke's Aussie guard, Jessica Foley, a player who chose Duke over UCONN because of its reputedly superior academics. In response to Foley's explanation of her choice of schools, Coach Auriemma was quoted as having said that as many Duke graduates waited tables as did graduates from other schools. The Crazies would not let him forget his words. One sign in the crowd read "Tonight's Special . . . Humble Pie for Auriemma and UCONN."

The UCONN coach had been right about one thing: the Duke team was less prepared for the spotlight than his team was. The first half seemed to prove this. The Blue Devils were dominated by Connecticut, trailing at the half 41-20. Shortly into the second half, that margin grew to 28 points. But the Duke team's determination showed when they rallied over the final ten minutes to bring the score close. Twice within the final two minutes, UCONN's lead decreased to single digits. And the fans in Cameron were going crazy. The noise they made shook the stadium in anticipation of a Duke win.

Much to the disappointment of the fans, the Huskies were eventually triumphant, defeating Duke 77-65. But that game should have proved one thing to the students. All those excuses about women's basketball not being exciting couldn't be more false. Not only was the play by UCONN extremely impressive, but so too was the resilience and determination of the Duke women during their comeback. The fans' appreciation for the Blue Devils' second-half surge made for some of the loudest moments ever heard inside of Cameron, as the entire stadium cheered the Duke team on.

The UCONN game, although not a win, was still a victory for the women's program. The three dominant excuses for not attending women's basketball games had all been negated. First, the lack-of-time excuse was disproved: the UCONN game drew enough enthusiasm, even in the height of tenting season, to incite students to take on extra tent shifts, and officials were even forced to turn fans away. People were willing to make time for this game, so why not others? Second, the women's team is not always guaranteed a win at home. We all wish the game against UCONN had not proved this point, but maybe if our team had as good a group of fans show up on a regular basis they would be prepared for the experience of playing to an audience. And last, the idea that a women's game just isn't as much fun is absolutely absurd. The game itself is only part of what makes watching basketball at Duke so exciting. The fans are what make Cameron so special. That's why the Crazies are hailed as the best "sixth man" (or "sixth woman," in this case) in basketball. The atmosphere inside the stadium is created by the students. The communal euphoria among the crowd during an exciting moment or after an important victory is the reason that so many people cram into the stadium. Conversely, the experience of failure also serves its purpose. When the team falls, so too do its fans, and that's where you see the true glory of Duke basketball and Cameron. After the women were defeated by the Huskies, the students may have been disappointed with the loss. But more important, they were proud of the program and their fellow students who refused to quit by mounting an impressive rally in the final minutes. In so doing, the women's team represented the indefatigable Duke spirit.

A true fan is a fan for life. I hope that the 2003 game against uconn brought more attention to the women's program at Duke and that will translate into more sustained support for the team. Remember that the atmosphere created by the students is just as important as the game is, and the combination of the two is what makes going to Cameron so much fun. And so, allow me to end with a simple request: Please, come out and support Duke's women players.

THE PRE-MED STUDENT

When the Women's Studies Major had ended her lecture about the importance of supporting both men's and women's basketball, the Host turned to her and said, "I don't think anyone here can argue with your point. But I should mention that, according to my research, fans of the Duke women lead the ACC in attendance. However, I'll be the first to admit that when I was a student here, I rarely turned out in support of both programs." Some of the tenters agreed with our Host, while others tried to make more excuses about why they wouldn't show up for both teams. Arguments began to break out, and finally, our Host decided to change the topic.

"Now, let's see," began the Host, "who would next like to make his or her story known? We're coming down to the last of this tent. Our variety is growing thin. Maybe we should ask our pre-med friend to tell us a good story." The Host looked at the Pre-Med Student, a double major in chemistry and biology, and asked, "Would you be so kind as to tell your tale next? You do, after all, seem like a devoted fan. Despite your need to take difficult classes and to participate in extracurricular activities in order to polish your medical school applications, I gather you don't miss many games. You must have something interesting to relate from all of your experiences. However, please keep in mind that these stories should be about Krzyzewskiville, and not about other tenters. We've seen how poorly the latter kind of tale has gone over."

"I have always found time for Duke basketball," the Pre-Med student replied, "but I'm not much of a storyteller—my specialties being in the sciences—so my recounting of the past won't be nearly as exciting as what we've heard from others. In consideration of the terms of our competition, I'll try to stick to the topic of K-ville, but first, since I have the floor, I'd like to reply to the concerns presented in the previous story. I might not have been to as many women's basketball games as I should have in my time at Duke, but, for what's it's worth, I'm always up to date with how our team does. When they're playing a game, I keep up with the score. I wish more games were televised. I would rather watch them play than be forced to use the Internet to check the score every few minutes—but that won't happen until TV coverage expands to incorporate more women's games. If it's any consolation, I've seen every women's game aired on television since I've been a student, and I've even followed them to the Final Four in Atlanta. I care as much about the success of their program as I do about the men's, and in retrospect, I'm sorry I haven't shown my appreciation as well as I should have, particularly in the years before they became a dominant program.

"Nevertheless, I'll get on with my story because I can see that our journalist friend is getting annoyed with my delay in the game. What he doesn't realize is that I've brought us toward the theme of my tale. It's a tale of appreciation of the basketball program for the sake of the team members as our fellow students, and not for the glory the players earn for our school.

THE PRE-MED STUDENT

IS INTERRUPTED BY

AN UNEXPECTED GUEST

Just as the Pre-Med Student was about to begin her story, a voice outside the tent interrupted. "Anyone in there?" the unseen visitor asked.

"Come on in!" answered the Captain as we all turned toward the entrance.

"I thought I heard voices in here," he said, as he removed his shoes and entered the tent.

"What are you doing here?" asked our Captain. "Are you about to call a check?" Upon hearing this second question, I knew why the visitor seemed familiar; I hadn't been used to seeing him in K-ville without the uniform blue-nylon jacket that the people in his position wear. He was one of the line monitors.

"Don't you wish," he answered with a sly chuckle, and the hopeful look on the Captain's face vanished.

The other tenters must have realized that our visitor was one of the line monitors as well, because no sooner had he squeezed into the circle between the Captain and the Freshman did my

148

tent mates begin to bombard him with questions. "When are you calling the next check?" asked the Math Major and the Pre-Law Student nearly simultaneously.

"Why are you out here if you're not about to call one?" added the Public Policy Major.

"They're not going to have us all stand out there in the rain, are they?" questioned the Pre-Med Student.

"They're not going to send us home just because of a little water, right?" asked the Freshman.

"You know I can't tell you when the next check is," answered the Line Monitor. "It could be three minutes from now, or in three hours."

"Wait a minute," said our Host at last, who had, up to this point, been merely looking in on the conversation. "Who is this person, and why would he know when the personal checks are going to be called?"

"Oh, I'm sorry," answered the Captain. "This is my friend Randy; he's one of the line monitors." He then turned to his friend and added, "And this is Rodney, a reporter who's been sitting in the tent with us tonight in order to learn more about K-ville."

"A line monitor!" exclaimed the Host. "This is wonderful. Do you mind if I ask you some questions?"

"I don't see why not."

"Great," chimed the Host as he flipped the page of his note-book and scrawled a few hurried marks. "First, let me just ask something out of my curiosity. Since you're a line monitor, you don't have to be out here except to call the personal checks, right? So why are you out here right now? Unless, of course, you're about to call one, which I suppose could be the case."

The Line Monitor shrugged and said, "Why not come out here? Just because I'm a line monitor doesn't mean that I don't like spending time in Krzyzewskiville. I was a tenter for two years before doing this, and I know that K-ville on the nights of personal checks is one of the best places to be on campus. This is where the party's at."

"Except for tonight," huffed the Sociology Major.

"True," continued the Line Monitor. "This rain has put a damper on the fun. But still, I figured it would be a good idea to come out to K-ville for at least a little while. You see, most tenters think that the line monitors don't do anything to deserve their place in line. So sometimes it's a good idea to hang out in K-ville to both show that we're out here too, and to get to know the tenters. Since I know some of the people in this tent, and heard voices as I walked by, I figured I would get out of the rain for a few minutes and come say hi."

"Okay," said our Host, "that makes sense. Some of these guys were making it sound as though line monitors don't come to K-ville except to call checks and to take their prime seats for the games."

"I know that's what some people think of us, but we do our share of work too."

"Really? Like what?" asked the Women's Studies Major.

"I'll be the first person to admit that being a line monitor isn't necessarily as much work as tenting, but we do a lot of stuff behind the scenes."

"Can you be a bit more specific?" questioned our Host.

"Well," began the Line Monitor, "our primary responsibility is, of course, to call tent checks. I know that from an outsider's perspective, calling checks seems much easier than tenting. I'll grant you the time commitment isn't as great, but conducting tent checks is actually far more inconvenient than just making them. Back when I had tent shifts, I would dread going outside; but once I was settled in my tent, I had a good two hours to do whatever I wanted—read, write, watch a movie, maybe take a nap. As a line monitor, when I'm assigned to call a tent check I have to put down whatever I'm doing, make my way over to K-ville, wait around for other line monitors to show up, call the check, mark everyone off, and then go back to my room or wherever else I might have come from. I spend a good thirty or forty-five minutes, whereas a tenter is able to stay productive."

"You can't be serious." asked the Pre-Law Student. "You're trying to convince us that having to call a check is more difficult than tenting because it interrupts your life? Do you mean to tell me that having to block off two hours of my day isn't as much of an interruption?"

"Wait, you didn't let me finish," said the Line Monitor. "I was just beginning. Now, imagine if one of these checks is at three in the morning. That means that I have to set my alarm for 2:45, wake up in the middle of the night, put some clothes on, leave my warm room and stumble out to K-ville, and then stand there in the freezing cold through the entire check while everyone else gets to leave as soon as we've checked them off."

At that moment a pillow flew across the tent and into the Line Monitor's face—a response from the Sociology Major. The Line Monitor pushed the pillow aside with a laugh and then said, "Okay, I suppose I deserved that. Somehow I can never convince anyone that we do enough to earn our seats for the games. But remember: beyond tent checks we have other responsibilities as well, including regular meetings where we plan events, discuss problems, and take care of the general organization of K-ville. Line monitors are in constant contact with administrators, the media, the basketball program, and other similar groups. Whenever tenters are given free food or a band comes out to K-ville, it was the line monitors who arranged it."

"To be honest," began the Host, "as an outsider to this tenting process, I can see the need for line monitors, but you haven't convinced me that they deserve some of the best seats in Cameron." The Line Monitor tried to interrupt, but our Host spoke on. "But I have an idea to give you one more chance. We've been entertaining ourselves this evening by way of a storytelling competition featuring tales of Krzyzewskiville. If you're interested, and the rest of our company agrees, would you care to join the game and tell us a story featuring your own experiences as a line monitor? Perhaps then you will convince us of how important the line monitors are to K-ville."

"Yes!" exclaimed the Economics Major, "he should definitely join our competition. I want to hear something about K-ville from a line monitor's perspective."

The rest of us agreed except for the Math Major, who made an excellent point when he said, "Of course, we don't want to be keeping you from anything else you may have to be doing right now." He gave the Line Monitor a hopeful smile.

"Oh, I have time for a story," said the Line Monitor, after which a number of our company sighed heavily. "And I think last night gave me the perfect story to demonstrate just what kinds of things we line monitors have to deal with."

Here We Learn of the Experience of the Line Monitor

I was sitting at my desk doing homework as the time neared for us to call last night's first personal check. As all of you know, we called the check at midnight, so this was probably 11:40. Before a personal check, the line monitors gather in a secret location, away from K-ville, which is different for each of the five checks. We then walk out to the tenters as a group.

I decided I better start getting ready, so I put on my shoes and grabbed my line monitor jacket. I couldn't wear it, of course; I didn't want people seeing me with it on, or else they might realize that we were about to conduct a check and run out to K-ville just in time to make it. But when I opened my door and stepped into the hall, I noticed that people poked their heads out of their rooms to see if it was me who was leaving. Many began hurriedly putting clothes on, and it occurred to me that my hall mates — most of whom are tenters — had all been waiting for me to leave my room before they went out to K-ville.

I couldn't let them cheat their way into the game, so I pretended to be going to the bathroom and made sure that everyone saw me walking back into my room. Lucky for me, my room is on the ground floor of the residence hall, and I was able to pop open the screen and squeeze through the open window while the rest of my hall mates thought I was still sitting in my room.

Outside in the cold air, I sneaked toward the rendezvous point, which was the baseball field. I thought about putting on my jacket, but I noticed that there were too many people walking around campus. What if one of them recognized the jacket and realized that we were about to hold a personal check? I couldn't have people calling up all their friends and warning them that we were coming. I strode toward the other line monitors, but without my jacket on, it sure was cold.

The best way to get to the baseball field from West Campus is to cut straight through K-ville. However, since many tenters now recognize me — as everyone here proved when I entered earlier — you could probably guess that I couldn't exactly just walk through the heart of the tent city if I was trying to be secretive. But I'm a pretty lazy guy, and it was cold, so I decided I would just cut through the woods running alongside of K-ville and Cameron.

Now, I probably should have taken the long way around — it

might have taken more time, but at least I would have reached the meeting place without looking like I had just come from a battlefield. Cutting through the woods in the dark had left me torn and tattered. Here, I'll pull up the leg of my pants to show you. Do you see all the cuts from the thorns and branches? And look at this one above my eye. Just think, an inch lower and I could have been blinded for life! Do you see the kinds of trials we, as line monitors, have to endure simply to do our jobs? Now are you beginning to understand the kind of work that goes into overseeing the line?

Once I reached the meeting place, and all of the other line monitors had arrived, we were each assigned our responsibilities. Of course, I wanted to be the person to blow the siren — everyone loves that guy. You would be surprised at just how many drunken hugs he gets as he walks around with the bullhorn. But someone else took that job, so I volunteered to hold one of the lists and check people off. No such luck there, either; all of the clipboards were taken before I could grab one myself. That left me with the worst assignment at a personal check.

"Okay, whoever doesn't have a job," began the head line monitor, "I need you guys to stop runners." He then assigned two people to the position next to Cameron and two at the other entrance to K-ville by the IM Building. Two other line monitors and I were assigned to the hardest place to guard runners — at the entrance to the parking lot off Towerview Drive.

"Towerview?" my friend Jacob complained. "I don't want to have to stop people from running out to K-ville up there. Once everyone starts calling their friends and telling them about the check, three of us are going to have to try to stop fifty kids."

"Fifty drunk kids," added Blake, the third of us assigned to Towerview.

"It's only midnight," I suggested, "maybe they aren't that drunk yet."

The three of us broke out into laughter. "You wish," said Jacob. "Now come on, we've got to get over to Towerview before they blow the siren."

We were about halfway to the road when we heard the wail of the siren coming from the direction of K-ville. I shouted, "Come on! Let's hurry! All the cell phones are probably coming out." We reached the road and Jacob took the farthest position by the tennis stadium, Blake stayed back at the edge of the woods and the road, and I got stuck at the middle post where the crosswalk connects main West Campus and the athletic facilities.

Not a minute had passed before the first of the runners came into view beneath the archways on West. But as soon as this group saw me standing in their path, they turned around. I looked to my right and saw a group of five kids running toward Jacob. As soon as they crossed Towerview he stepped in front of them and held them up. Two more students came in my direction, but again they saw me and thought twice about approaching. This time, however, instead of turning around and going back to their rooms, these kids veered to the left and started jogging toward the woods. Blake ran after them, and I moved over to cover his position as well.

Five or six more students came running from the dorms, but they all turned around as soon as they saw me. Whether they went home or whether they tried to get into K-ville from some other entrance is a good question. All I knew is that at least I didn't have to deal with them.

But when a group of three obviously drunk guys started staggering toward me while trying to avoid looking in my direction, I knew that I was about to have a problem. "Where are you guys headed?" I questioned them as soon as they had crossed over Towerview. "You know I can't let you go out there while they're having a check. You're going to have to wait here for a few minutes."

"No man, we've been out there for a while," said the first one, a tall brunet who looked like he had spent a good bit of time in the gym. Come to think of it, all three of them were pretty big guys, especially compared to me. But I wasn't afraid of them. I had my blue jacket, and I had the position of power.

"If you've been out there for a while, why are you coming from the residential quads?" I asked, skeptical of the excuse that would inevitably ensue.

"We just had to run to the library," said another one of the guys.

"Do you guys always go to the library drunk?" I asked them while still blocking their path. The third one, who appeared to be talking on a cell phone, tried to walk around his two friends and me. "Hold on," I told him, "you're going to have to wait right here."

"Dude, I'm on the phone," he said as he kept walking.

I put my hand out to stop him, and he grabbed my wrist. I looked at him levelly and said, "First, don't you dare touch me. Second, you three better turn around and walk on back to the dorms." We stared at each other in silence for about thirty seconds before he let go of my arm, and he and his friends started walking back toward the residential quads.

Just when I thought I was done with those kids they turned to their left and began moving up Towerview toward the woods. "Damn it!" I thought to myself as I drifted in the same direction. I had to watch them, but at the same time, I didn't want to leave my post at the crosswalk.

The three drunken boys loitered at the edge of the forest for a few minutes while I hid in the shadows of a nearby tree watching to see what they would do next. Just as I had suspected, without any warning they sprinted into the woods, and I took off after them.

They wanted to cut through the woods and sneak into K-ville, but I'm no idiot; I wasn't about to try to chase them through the trees in the dark. I had already walked through there earlier in the night, and I wasn't about to do it again, this time in a full-out run. I cut through the parking lot, keeping my eyes on all three shadows dashing through the brush; then I positioned myself between K-ville and the forest, waiting for the runners to come sneaking out.

They each broke out of the woods at a different place, but I was standing in a position that allowed me to see all three of them. The disadvantage of that spot was that they could all see me as well, and they all emerged and headed in different directions.

I called to a fellow line monitor, "Hey, do you see that kid coming out of the woods up there? Make sure you stop him. Don't let him into the check!" She started moving in the farthest runner's direction as I positioned myself between the two others, trying to keep track of both of them.

The two students I was still after were the first and third boys I had stopped—that would be the tall brunet and the one with the cell phone, for those of you not keeping up. I was especially determined to get the kid with the cell phone, but he was walking in the opposite direction of the line monitors performing the check. On the other hand, the first guy was heading toward the rest of the tenters, and I couldn't let him walk straight into the check while his friend moved further from the checklists. I memorized the blue ski jacket of the cell phone kid—it had a yellow stripe across the chest and back—and began tailing the tall brunet.

He weaved in between the maze of tents as I followed. I tried to stay back and out of his sight to make him think he lost me, and eventually, it worked. He made his way over to the rest of his tent mates and the line monitor performing his check. As he walked toward the large group of students surrounding the line monitor, I cut him off and said, "Don't even think about trying to make this check."

All of his friends and tent mates were standing nearby and

saw the confrontation. They looked on, laughing because they knew that I had caught him. "But I've been out here all night," he tried to convince me again.

I pointed in the direction of the head line monitor and said, "That's not my problem. If you want to complain to someone, go talk to him." We scowled at each other for a few moments, and then he muttered a few expletives and stormed off in the direction of the head line monitor.

Now that I had stopped him, it was time to see if I could find the cell phone kid. I assumed that the three runners belonged to the same tent, and by following the first guy I had a good feeling that I might have figured out where to find the one I really wanted to catch.

I slipped into the crowd surrounding the line monitor who would be calling his tent, and I waited to see if my target would appear. At last, as the line monitor called for Tent 58, that familiar blue ski jacket with the yellow stripe came into view, and I prepared to pounce. When he approached the line monitor, holding out his ID card, I stepped out from the crowd and snatched it from him, saying, "I don't think so. You're not going to be making this check, or any check for that matter. I'm kicking you out of the line. Get out of K-ville."

He looked as though he was about to punch me, but I refused to back down. I'll admit that I was scared; after all, he was much bigger than me. But on the other hand, I knew that he wouldn't dare touch me considering the possible consequences.

If he were to hit me, suddenly not going to the Carolina game would become the least of his worries.

He huffed away in disgust while I stood in the center of the crowd of tenters, all of whom were applauding my heroic efforts to stand up to those kids that think they're too good to follow the rules of the system.

Here Follows an Epilogue to
the Line Monitor's Tale

When the line monitor had completed his heroic tale, we were all a bit skeptical. The Women's Studies Major spoke up, saying "Really? Everyone around you applauded for kicking some random boy out of K-ville? I highly doubt that."

"Well," began the Line Monitor, "Maybe that's not exactly how the story ended. There was no applause, and actually I probably looked like a big jerk, but what people need to understand is that I was just doing my job. As a line monitor, I'm out here to monitor the line and make sure people are playing by the rules. I hate how mad people get when we simply do our job of enforcement. If you miss two checks and we have to bump you to the back of the line, even if it's the night before the game, you can't be mad at us because it was your tent's fault that you missed the check.

"People should be thanking us for enforcing the regulations. Without me doing my job, someone like that guy with the cell phone—a person who tried to cheat the system and not stay out here in K-ville—might be let in before a more deserving student who followed all of the rules.

"And while I'm thinking about it, let me also add that we're tired of hearing tenters complain about the line monitors making it too hard on you guys. Remember that everyone out here opted to tent; we didn't force you to do it. You're supposed to be earning your spot through dedication and sacrifice—not tenting only under the most ideal of circumstances. Our job, as line monitors, is to make sure that people don't try to bypass that aspect; we're not here to make tenting easier."

"Interesting to hear the other perspective, isn't it?" asked the Host. "All night long I've been hearing complaints about the line monitors, but I can see that they have troubles to deal with as well."

"Wait just one second," interrupted the Pre-Law Student. "Now, I can understand that the line monitors have to deal with certain problems of their own, but you can't convince me that being a line monitor is more work than being a tenter."

"I made no such claim," sighed the exasperated Line Monitor. "I simply wanted to point out that we do our share of work. Honestly, at how many tent checks have you been threatened with physical violence?"

"Oh, don't exaggerate," the Public Policy Major chimed in.

"Come now," declared our Host, "That was a wonderful story to hear. Let's not ruin it with this foolish bickering. Back to our game—we've still got more tales to go, and if I remember correctly, we were interrupted just as one was getting under way."

Before resuming with the Pre-Med Student's tale, the Host turned to the Line Monitor and said, "We have four more stories to get through before everyone in this company has told his or her tale. You're certainly welcome to stay and listen in . . . assuming, of course, that you have enough time."

"I'd love to," answered the Line Monitor (to a chorus of groans, I might add).

THE PRE-MED STUDENT
CONTINUES HER PROLOGUE

The Host looked toward the Pre-Med Student and asked, "Where did we leave off?"

"Now," said the Pre-Med Student, "as I was saying, the tale I'm about to begin will discuss appreciation of the basketball program for the sake of our fellow students on the team. My story addresses a troubling characteristic of the Cameron Crazies that I began to notice this past year. It seems like students are more concerned with looking and acting crazy for the media than they are with cheering on our team or intimidating the visitor. The Cameron Crazies have become nothing more than 'media whores.' They'll yell and scream, paint themselves all sorts of colors, wear foolish hats, and do just about anything else they can think of in order to get on camera. I might take part in my own share of foolish antics, but I do so to distract the opponent, not to be on television. Maybe it's just my opinion, but there seems to be something wrong with this practice. Why do the students feel a need to be the center of attention? It's as though they're trying to exploit their notoriety as avid fans to turn attention to themselves—not to help Duke win. Don't they realize that the important thing going on in Cameron is the basketball game, not their five seconds of fame?"

This message of selling out to expectations seemed like an ironic preface to the Pre-Med Student's tale, considering her chosen academic path. Then again, who am I to judge others' calculating methods to achieve success? Nevertheless, as promised, I shall now retell her tale here.

HERE FOLLOWS THE PRE-MED STUDENT'S TALE

"What do you suppose is happening up there?" asked Jason of his best friend, Zack. His attention was focused on a large and raucous crowd of Crazies gathered at the front of the walk-up line a couple of hours prior to tip-off.

"I'm not sure," said Zack. "I'll bet some of the opposing team's fans are walking by Cameron."

Jason continued to watch the crowd grow larger. After five minutes had passed, he looked back toward Zack and said, "I don't think so. They've been at it now for quite a while."

"It's a big game. They're probably just psyching themselves up."

"I think there's something else going on," said Jason. "Stay here. I'm going to go check it out."

Zack rolled his eyes, but Jason began to walk toward Cameron. "Don't worry," called Zack. "I'll just wait here and . . . um . . . save your place."

Jason maneuvered the obstacle course now covering the sidewalk. He stepped in between groups of friends chatting, around chairs with people reading, and over sleeping bags filled by students. He reached the crowd gathered at the front of K-ville, and pushed his way toward the center of the circle of curious onlookers, where he discovered a group of students preparing for the game by painting their bodies blue. Anyone who has been around Cameron before a game knows that such antics don't constitute an unusual sight. However, in this particular instance, a television camera was taping the students.

Catching sight of the camera, Jason thought to himself, Where there's a camera there's almost always a reporter. He looked around for someone holding a microphone, but he saw no one. Instead, focusing his attention on the students covering each other in blue, he realized that one of them was much older than the others, and perhaps not a student at all. This tall, thin woman with long brunette hair was wearing gray shorts and a blue sports bra. At first glance she might have passed for a student, but Jason had noticed a thin, black wire running up her back and to a personal microphone clipped to the strap over her shoulder. He thought it odd to see such a device on one of the tenters. When he caught the eye of the person watching the spectacle next to him, he asked, "What's going on here?"

"I think one of the sports networks is doing a special piece on the Crazies," answered the boy at his side. "That lady on the right, the one in the gray shorts, she's a reporter."

To Jason's left, a girl added, "They seem to do at least one story like this every year."

"I've seen them report on the antics of the Crazies," said Jason, "but I've never seen a journalist go quite as far as joining in with the students. I'll bet she gets a nice bonus for this. It can't be more than forty degrees out here." The three of them laughed while they continued to watch the clearly ambitious journalist paint herself blue in order to get her story about fanatic college students.

When he returned to his place in line with Zack, Jason revealed to his friend the cause of the commotion at the front of the queue. Zack gave a condescending reply, saying, "Stupid media whores. Why are these kids so quick to sell out? Can't they just be excited about Duke basketball?"

At the next home game Jason and Zack encountered media whoredom in the heart of Cameron. With an hour to go before tip-off, the players were in the locker rooms and the cameras were on the hardwood taping the pregame show. Two commentators sat on stools in the center of Coach K Court. In the background stood the Cameron Crazies, mentally preparing for the approaching game.

An employee of the broadcasting company came over to the student section and asked for the students to cheer when she signaled to them. Like trained monkeys, come the woman's signal, the Crazies started yelling. Such a response just once would have been fine; perhaps twice would have been acceptable too. But the media lady kept making the signal, and each time the students went crazy. Zack turned to Jason, obviously angry, and said "I can't believe the students are so quick to play up to the media."

The next time the Crazies were signaled, Zack and Jason yelled to their peers, "Don't do it!" and "Quiet down!" Few people paid attention, and the fans continued to scream for the cameras. Jason shrugged and said, "Soon the media will be trying to put a copyright on Krzyzewskiville."

Watching television later that same week, Jason and Zack saw a commercial exploiting the antics of the Crazies in order to promote the network's college basketball coverage. Specifically, it was being used to advertise an upcoming Duke game, and part of the advertisement showed the Cameron Crazies crowd surfing Dick Vitale around the student section. "That's it!" exclaimed Zack. "This is getting ridiculous. We can't let the media continue to benefit from the enthusiasm of our fans."

"Zack," interrupted Jason, "who cares? It's just kids having fun."

"They can have fun all they want," argued Zack, "but the

students need to remember that we're there for the game, not the damn cameras. I'm tired of seeing networks take advantage of our school spirit for their ratings."

"But they're just advertising Duke games," explained Jason. "We want people to watch them."

"Okay, then show highlights from a game. Show a big slam dunk! People are supposed to be watching the action on the court, not the fans in the stands. More importantly, the students shouldn't be playing toward the cameras. They should be distracting the other team."

"Well, what are you planning on doing about it?"

Zack hesitated for a moment, and then said, "I'll come up with something, don't worry."

Before the next nationally televised game, Jason asked, "Yo, Zack, you want to grab some food before the game?"

"I've got a meeting," answered Zack. "Don't wait up for me — I'm sure you'll see me at the game."

Having forgotten Zack's earlier words of frustration, Jason thought nothing of his friend's excuse for being late to the game. He entered Cameron with a group of his hall-mates and they found a spot along the foul line, five rows back on the TV side of the student section. A pregame show was in progress again, and as before, the cameras were taping two announcers at center court. One of the network representatives came over and told the Crazies to watch for her signal to start cheering. The crowd watched and awaited her sign.

The network representative flashed her signal, and the Crazies started cheering—but not for her. Zack jumped onto the press table at center court wearing a full length tan trench coat. On his face was the letter *D* painted in white. When he threw off his coat, everyone could see that his body was plastered with newspapers.

"What am I?" yelled Zack to the jubilant crowd, waving his arms and running back and forth across the press table.

The response from the group around him had been planned. The first few rows of students shouted out the answer, "Media whore!" But they didn't stop there; that would have been too tactful for the Cameron Crazies. Instead, the students started chanting "Media whore, media whore"—for the television cameras! As they yelled the words, which I'm sure the microphones picked up, Zack jumped onto the court and ran in circles behind the announcers until a group of security officers pulled him out of the stadium.

After the game, Jason knocked on Zack's door. When it opened, he saw his best friend back in blue-jeans and a t-shirt, his face washed of all the white paint, carrying a garbage bag filled with crumpled newspapers. The two friends stared at each other in silence until they simultaneously broke into laughter.

Five minutes passed before the two could speak. When they had calmed down, Jason said, "You know something, Zack, I don't think you were very successful."

"Why is that?" he asked.

"Well, you gave the media exactly what they wanted."

"What do you mean?"

"They might not have thought so at the time, but your stunt was perfect for them. They always rave about the antics of the Cameron Crazies, and you just gave them a perfect example of why. I was just watching some game highlights and they showed a clip of your little stunt before the game."

Zack smiled at Jason and then confided to his friend. "I never said I wasn't a media whore as well."

The Pre-Med Student's story surprised us with its comedic appeal. Everyone seemed to enjoy it, except for our Host, the journalist. "That's not fair," he said after setting aside his pad in mock disgust.

"It's not fair that the television cameras try to exploit the students?"

"You have to look at it from our perspective," explained the Host. "The relationship with the media is important both for us and for the school. For my newspaper or for a television station, I'll admit that yes, we use the Cameron Crazies to sell our product. But at the same time, by giving publicity to the student body, we're giving great publicity to the school."

The Pre-Med Student still looked cynical. She shook her head and asked, "But can't the media publicize other things? Why focus on the oddities of our style of cheering? There are students here making medical discoveries, writing books, or even volunteering to teach kids at local schools. Why not talk more about them? It's not that I expect the system to change completely; after all, sports sell a lot better than stories about kids being active in their communities. But I just wish people would get their priorities in order."

Our Host thought for a moment before responding. He then lifted up his pad and wrote down a brief note before saying, "I do agree that there are some great things going on at this school, as well as at every other university around the nation. But part of the allure of writing about the Cameron Crazies is that they're the kids who are researchers and scholars, and who knows, maybe they made an important discovery while tenting for a basketball game. It's a future doctor or lawyer who is painted blue and wearing a cape."

"Well, the moral of my story is obvious," she replied, "but I'm also willing to admit that playing to the media isn't entirely bad, as I think we're perhaps proving tonight by helping our new acquaintance to understand the true spirit of K-ville. However, I think there's one thing television forces us to do which, I'll argue, hurts Cameron. Everyone gets in line early for the best seats in the house. We designate these seats to be on what's called the TV side of the stadium, the side across from the player's benches which is shown most often when the cameras are filming a game. But doesn't the name itself touch on the problem we're having? We call one side the TV side, meaning that if we sit over there, we have a better chance of showing up on television. This is especially true if we cover our entire body in blue paint. That's what the viewers like to see, so that's what the cameras show. But another reason for sitting on the TV side that I've always heard, and the reason that served as my motive for telling my story, is that it's more exciting on that side of the stadium. The fans are louder and more spirited. As a result, the games are more fun to watch and the cheers are more fun to take part in.

"Now, imagine this. What if some of the really hard-core fans made it a point to sit on the non-TV side?" The tenters began immediately to express their opinions, but the Pre-Med Student shushed them. She said, "I think one of the reasons the TV side is more fun than the other has something to do with the fact that everyone's louder. But if we brought some of those people who are willing to yell to the other side, they could encourage the traditionally quieter section to get into the game. By doing this the entire experience could become that much more exciting and beneficial to the team.

"The buffer zone of resident advisors and special guests behind the opponent's bench, for example, exists today because of a selective living group that went by the name Bunch of Guys, or BOG for short, which no longer exists on campus. Every game they'd arrive early to get the seats directly behind the opposing team's bench. During time-outs they would yell as loud as they could—the result being, of course, that the opponent couldn't have an effective huddle because there would be no way to hear each other or the coach over the noise.

"I think if we can get those kinds of outgoing students, the ones who aren't afraid to yell at the top of their lungs, on both sides of the court, we'll be able to improve on the already amazing experience of watching a basketball game in Cameron."

"That's a great idea," the Host said. "I was here during the time of BOG, and I remember seeing teams forced to move their time-out huddles onto the court. I honestly think you're right because I know how effective those kids were. But I have one question for you. Are you willing to sit on the non-TV side?" The Pre-Med student's cheeks turned red when asked this question. The Host continued, saying, "I think you'll be hard pressed to find students willing to wait in line for months just to make sure they get seats in a section where it's not as fun to watch the games."

"But that's my point," pleaded the Pre-Med Student, "once we can get people to switch sides, both sides should be equally as exciting." She shook her head and pulled her knees up to her chest. Then, with a tone of feigned indifference, the Pre-Med Student made her final remark. "I realize that it probably won't happen, but maybe we, as a tent, should think about trying it."

I'm ashamed to admit that most of my fellow tenters argued in disagreement. I doubt they did so because they didn't agree with the idea; I think they just weren't willing to risk their seats on the TV side. Her idea did make sense. In my opinion, it's the fans that make the TV side the better side to be on for a game, not the television cameras. If we could just get that same enthusiasm into the other side by way of a loud group of fans, it wouldn't matter what side you sit on for a game because the energy would be all around Cameron. I, for one, would be willing to give it a try so long as I knew that I could get other equally enthusiastic people to come to the non-TV side.

"Apparently, your tent mates might need some convincing," remarked our Host to the Pre-Med Student, "but I'm willing to bet that if they tried your idea once, they would see the benefit of their experiment, and it wouldn't take too much work to convince them to switch sides again."

"I'm willing," murmured the Freshman.

In response to his shyness, the Math Major joked, "See, there's one student who will obviously help with loud cheers!"

The Captain tried to back up his little brother by saying, "Come on guys, I think it's a good idea too." However, the remainder of the tent had another laugh at the Freshman's expense. I daresay the evening's competition may have convinced him never again to speak in the presence of upperclassmen.

"Why don't we move the line monitor section to the non-TV side?" joked the Sociology Major. "After all, they're such dedicated fans."

The Line Monitor scowled at the Sociology Major from across the circle. "If Tent 25 should somehow get bumped," he threatened, "I guess they'd get to test out moving to the non-TV side sooner than expected."

The Host interrupted, bringing us back to the main focus of his storytelling contest. "Now, if you all have had your fun laughing at this dedicated student," he chided, "and perhaps one more dedicated than any of you," he added in response to the smirks creeping onto some of our faces, "let's get to the next person in line."

The Host looked at the Math Major and said, "Since you're so quick to joke about others, why don't we see what you have to offer? As a senior, you've certainly spent a lot of time in K-ville and Cameron. What can you tell us about this tradition?"

"Well, not to brag, but I know a good bit about the subject." The Math Major smirked, but his grin faded when he added, "However, it seems that everyone has covered a lot of the good stories I know. Perhaps if I had been able to go when first asked, I could have told something original." My anticipation subsided with his revelation; I had been curious to hear what kind of humorous story the jovial Math Major would tell us. Would one of our tenters get by without telling a tale? "But," he added, much to everyone's delight, "there's one aspect of K-ville that all of you seem to have forgotten."

THE MATH MAJOR'S TALE

"Being a Cameron Crazie isn't all fun and games," explained the Math Major, "it takes hours of practice, patience, sweat, and even blood to earn the distinction of being the best fans in the nation. People think that all we do is yell as loud as we can, but that's what fans from other schools do—not the Cameron Crazies. An uninformed outsider looking in doesn't realize the amount of training and preparation that goes into our game-time antics."

Everyone in the tent laughed at the Math Major's exaggerations, but he kept a straight face and continued, "I myself have spent countless hours working with my friends in the off-season to perfect our skills as fans. My story, then, will explain the kind of work that goes into the preparations of a Cameron Crazie. Cheering is a skill, just like any other, so practice can help you to improve dramatically. And just as with any other skill, the ability to cheer also deteriorates with lack of use. Off-season conditioning is the secret behind the success of Duke's 'sixth man.'"

When any sport's season ends for the year, the average fan makes the mistake of putting his or her fanaticism into hibernation until the games begin again. But the Cameron Crazies are not your average fans. When college basketball season ends, the players don't put their basketballs and high-tops into the closet for the summer. They train hard, hit the weights, work on their weaknesses, and hone their skills in order to come back faster, stronger, and better prepared to defend the winning tradition of Duke basketball. We too, as the country's best fans, must utilize the off-season if we expect to show improvement of our intimidation skills. The next year we need to be louder, wittier, haughtier, and better prepared to defend the formidable reputation of Cameron Indoor Stadium.

Last year's record no longer matters. Whether we won the NCAA Tournament or failed to qualify for the NIT, the first step to off-season conditioning requires the realization that last year is over. It ended at the final second of the season's last game. From that moment, everything becomes preparation for the challenges to come in the next season.

Don't misunderstand me. It's okay to take a few days off to recuperate, both physically and mentally. In fact, I recommend it. If you don't, you're liable to spend the next year over-cheering to compensate for last year's mistakes. You have to move forward. Get past a botched chant or a misplaced taunt that may have cost us a game. What's the first rule? Last year is over. It's in the past. Take a few days off and bask in the accomplishments of the prior year. Remember the free throw you made the Wake Forest player miss thanks to the flawless execution of a well-timed scream? What about that profanity you evoked from an opposing player, the one that led to a technical foul? Be proud of such events, but don't forget: nothing can be changed. Enjoy the successes of the season and forget the mistakes.

The recuperation period can last anywhere from a few days to a couple of weeks. But keep in mind, the longer you wait to practice game preparations, the harder it is to get back into shape. Once you've finished your relaxation and you're ready to get started again, avoid strenuous, hard-core cheering in the first few weeks. You have almost an entire year to get into condition. The body needs time to ease back into the strain of aggressive cheering—otherwise it may not make it through the next season. If the Crazies over-exert themselves, their enthusiasm will die down as the season progresses. By the time we reach senior night—the last home game of the season—Cameron will sound quieter than the Dean Dome over in Chapel Hill.

Start your conditioning at a moderate level. My recommendation is to hit the weights. At least three times a week, but no more than five—you want to work on gaining mass. Of course, during the season we can't afford to be sore, so the weight room is a dangerous place. Imagine trying to perform free-throw arm extensions after having done military presses: you would be lucky to raise your arms halfway! Watch a good free throw shooter. Notice how he follows the same routine before every shot. Cheering is all about routine. If you're sore you'll change your routine. That's when cheers begin to break down. During the off-season, when you don't have to worry about a game the next day, you can push yourself without worrying about strain.

There are a few muscle groups on which to focus once you hit the weights. Start with your upper body. I'm talking triceps, biceps, chest, and shoulders. These are the critical muscles for many of the cheers. For good, loud clapping, of course, you'll need strong triceps, but you might want to work the shoulders and chest as well. In addition to clapping, the "Let's Go, Duke" cheer requires fist pumping at increased speeds. To keep up with the rest of the Crazies, you're going to need well-toned arms and shoulders. Try this, it's one of my personal favorites. Take a weight. It doesn't have to be that heavy, maybe fifteen or twenty pounds. Hold it in your right hand and do fist pump sets of ten. After a few weeks of this, you'll find that your cheering has become both faster and crisper. Last, but not least, a powerful upper body is key for effective crowd surfing of other students and, occasionally, Dickie V. Don't be the weak link who can't support the weight of a fellow student or celebrity as he passes over your head. Get to the weight room and work those muscles.

The other area you want to hit hard in the weight room is the lower body. Pay special attention to the calves. They'll be the vital muscle group for increasing your opening tip-off vertical. Jumping rope might be your best bet here. No need for any of that one-foot crap. Keep it simple: use both feet and work on increasing height and speed. Also, and I can't stress this enough, pay attention to balance. If you're jumping rope somewhere, you're probably on a large, flat surface. But in Cameron you're on a small, wooden bleacher about six or eight inches wide. If you don't have good balance, you're liable to fall off the bleacher into another Crazie and cause a domino effect that could ripple through the entire student section. Perhaps you should try to find a fallen tree on which to jump rope. I recommend a tree that crosses a stream or a small ravine. This way, balance becomes as important to you as height and duration. I'll also note that, as a true fan, you'll be playing basketball with friends. In order to better imitate your favorite players, a good vertical is going to be key. Otherwise, how do you expect to be able to throw down tomahawk dunks over other people?

After a few weeks of just hitting the weight room, start incorporating some aerobic exercises. What activity you do is your own call. Personally, I like to run, but I've heard that swimming and biking are good alternatives. The low impact is supposedly better on your knees. Just keep in mind the reason behind your exercises. Everything aerobic is going to build endurance. What you want is an exercise that's also going to help you stand for the entire two hours of the basketball game, not to mention the hour, minimum, you're going to spend waiting on your feet before tip-off. I've seen it happen time and time again. We get a really good crop of freshman talent in, but they just don't have the endurance level necessary to actively participate through the entire game. Midway through the second half they're looking to sit down, but everyone knows there's no sitting in the student section of Cameron. It's a sign of weakness, and we can't afford to give the other team any indication of that. If we do, they'll eat us alive out there. That's unacceptable.

Now, I've spent all of this time talking about exercise, but diet is just as important. Part of the basketball experience is working around a college student's schedule. This means fast food and pizza all the time. Now, let's be realistic. How many of us have time to eat healthy? No one. We're Duke students. We run from class to class, to club, to community service, and in between we may have enough time to pick up a burger and fries. Now, if you go home for the summer, you're likely to revert to good, healthy, home-cooked meals, which means that you won't be able to handle the rigors of a college student's diet once you return to campus. The key is pizza, at least once a week — but more if you can pull it off. And always, always carry junk food with you. I can't stress that enough. I don't care if you're a chocolate person or a fruit-snacks lover — make sure you've got a package of candy on you at all times. Let your stomach know that you're not going to take it easy. You're not going to get soft on it by feeding it lettuce, or, heaven forbid, foods that aren't fried. Pretty soon, you'll be back to having pizza every night delivered to your tent in K-ville. What if you have an upset stomach? You can't risk missing a tent check or part of the game because you had to go to the bathroom. Your stomach needs to be able to handle greasy, sugary, fatty foods. Might I also add, as a side note, that those of you who like to celebrate with a bit of alcohol, don't worry about restricted access around your parents over the summer. The weightlifting is going to give you more mass. More mass leads to increased tolerance. As long as you stick to your exercise regimen, the number of beers you can drink while celebrating shouldn't decrease.

As the off-season progresses, you'll return to school in the fall. Lucky for us, football season is the perfect opportunity to start getting yourself back to your physical peak for Cameron. Why is this? Well, perhaps most important, a football game is going to last about three hours, versus two hours for a basketball game. If you can last through the football game on your feet, you should be fine come basketball season. But the key for football is to make sure that you find a spot in the front rows of the student section. Don't be one of those kids who arrive at the end of the first quarter and leaves at the half. Get to Wallace Wade Stadium early and stay through to the last second of the clock. It doesn't matter if we win or lose because you're there to practice your cheering technique. Taunting other schools' football players can be as much fun as mocking their basketball teams. For example, if they have a short, skinny kid who doesn't get playing time, whip out the classic "Ru-dy! Ru-dy!" If we're playing Florida State, taunt them with chants of "Wide Left." For NC State, yell "If you can't go to college go to State," or one of my favorites, "Big . . . High . . . School, Big-High-School." And of course, if the opponent is blowing us out of the water, shout "Go to Hell Carolina, Go to Hell!" (This, it should be noted, is technically valid at any time during any athletic event.) UNC is ultimately the only school we Crazies are concerned with. Football games should be no different. Make sure you let the other team know that.

Although, by winter break, basketball season has technically started, utilize these three or four weeks away from school for more Cameron Crazie conditioning. What you're going to want to focus on here is your K-ville preparations. Before the end of the fall semester, you should have already found the other members of your tent. If not, there's no time to waste. Get on it right away. Coming back from the holidays, you never know just when the rush to set up tents will begin. You won't have time to go looking for a group of people once you get back to school. In addition, all tenters need to spend the holidays getting supplies. Layers! Layers! Layers! I can't stress that enough. If you're going to be in a tent at night during the months of January and February, and you're more than thirty degrees above the equator, you need warm clothes. Because it will be winter break, you should have no problems finding gloves, snow hats, wool socks, heavy coats, ski masks, earmuffs, et cetera. You might feel foolish buying all of these things, but you'll thank me come the end of that first tent shift when you can still feel your fingers, ears, and nose.

If your group doesn't have a tent, winter is also the ideal time to buy one. The prices are low because nobody plans a camping trip in January. What you're looking for varies. Size always matters, right? We'll start there. You have twelve people in your group, but how often will all of you need to be in the tent at once? Only during personal checks, and even then, not everyone has to be out there. I recommend an eight-person tent. This should provide plenty of space. As far as color goes, the choice is yours. However, I suggest a tent that has a dark blue pattern on it to represent the school's colors and remind you why you're out here. Lastly, the most important aspect of your tent is going to be pole thickness. Trust me on this one, kids. If you try to cut corners, maybe save a couple of bucks by going to the local sells-everything-for-cheap store, you're only hurting yourself. You might be thinking that a tent is a tent as long as it keeps water out. But in the winter, you've got to deal with more than water. You've got ice and snow. Ice and snow gets heavy when it collects on top of your tent. After the first big snowstorm of the year, at least twenty tents collapse under the added weight because people saved a few dollars and wound up with thin little tent poles. It happens every time, and trust me, you don't want to be one of those people.

More important than the tent itself is how you pitch it. For this I must emphasize practice. Practice! Practice! Practice! Once you've bought a tent, practice setting it up at least five times a day. Do it more if you have the time. You might ask why. Well, I'll tell you: you're pitching a tent in winter, and since tents aren't often meant for winter weather, the structure has to be secure. For the same reason you need to be aware of tent-pole thickness, you have to be able to pitch your tent securely. The keys to avoiding tent collapse are a well-pitched tent and constant attention to ice removal. Come the end of the season, your tent will still be standing when all the others are flattened.

I remember freshman year when we were tenting amateurs. After the first ice storm, we had to go buy another tent. Two weeks later, the wind had picked up and since we hadn't properly secured the stakes, we found pieces of our new tent in four different places on campus. All these problems could have been avoided had we taken the time to practice pitching our tent.

If you've followed my instructions, come the beginning of basketball season late in the fall semester, you should physically be prepared to run the Cameron Crazie offense of cheers and jeers. Indeed, I've given you the tools to cheer longer, louder, and harder, and I've provided advice on how to stay sheltered and warm during the trials of tenting. Now we must move on to the substance behind the Cameron Crazies. I'm going to teach you how to be a better heckler.

Voice training is vital for the advanced heckler. Personally, after my freshman year I began to take voice lessons with a focus on opera. Now my voice is a well-oiled machine. It's all about pushing from the diaphragm. A lot of Crazies, new and veteran, try to scream from the throat. Not only does this method not allow you to produce as much sound as you can with the diaphragm, but it also cripples your voice. If you try to make it through a game at full strength from the throat, the next game you'll be useless. In addition, structure your breathing. Practice at home. Take a deep breath in for five seconds. Let it out for five seconds. Take a deep breath in for ten seconds. Let it out for ten seconds. Repeat. If you go into Cameron without proper breathing techniques, you'll be winded before the ten-minute mark. Remember, we're always making noise. In order to do that we must have exacting control of our voices.

To best practice heckling, use your surroundings. Everyone around you has something embarrassing that they don't want you to mention. The most obvious tool is a person's physical appearance. Maybe he or she has an ugly haircut. Maybe the person's clothes don't match. Be creative. Don't be afraid to say something witty or condescending about a thick pair of glasses. It will make the person stronger, and it will help you as you're screaming at an opponent on the free-throw line.

Another good source for ridicule is a person's name. Maybe you just met a guy named Jennifer, an obvious girl's name. Get in the guys face and say his name over and over again in an annoying voice. If you're punched because of it, at least you know that your chant was effective.

My final advice for chanting materials is to take full advantage of the Internet. I recommend doing random searches on the people you meet throughout the summer. You never know what you'll find. Maybe the person's been arrested a few times. Perhaps you can find old, nerdy-looking pictures of them. Everyone has something that embarrasses them, and there's a good chance that it's posted on the Internet. If nothing else, you'll probably be able to find the name of a mom, or sister, or dog. Chanting those names can still get under a person's skin. Also, talk to enemies. Ex-boyfriends or -girlfriends are a must. These people will always be able to provide you with private information that's both accurate and embarrassing. Once you've gathered the material, type the facts up on a sheet of paper, carry plenty of copies with you, and distribute them to other people when you're in a group with the person you intend to heckle. Create a good jeer from the list of facts you've accumulated. This method will work on improving your spontaneity and mocking abilities, skills that are paramount to an effective Cameron Crazie.

Allow me to offer a few words of caution before I conclude my discussion. Though heckling should be both funny and embarrassing, it should not be malicious. The Crazies are known for their wild antics but they are also sometimes considered cruel. Although an arrest for marijuana possession is comical and becomes perfect material for heckling, an alcohol addiction is not a subject to broach. In addition, stay away from the job security of a coach, the health of a player or player's relative, et cetera. Also, chants involving profanity should be avoided. Coach K dislikes obscene chants, and we should have more class than that and be more creative. Otherwise, we're no better than Maryland fans. For example, instead of using a chant which alludes to bovine excrement when a referee makes a bad call — like every other school in the country — be creative. In years past we've chanted phrases such as "I disagree," or "I beg to differ." Allow me, if I may, to quote from the now famous "Avuncular Letter" from the former Duke president Terry Sanford, or "Uncle Terry," as the student body knew him. He once made a request of the Cameron Crazies, saying:

Resorting to the use of obscenities in cheers and chants at ballgames indicates a lack of vocabulary, a lack of cleverness, a lack of ideas, a lack of class, and a lack of respect for other people. We are, I am sorry to report, gaining an unequal reputation as a student body that doesn't have a touch of class.

I don't think we need to be crude and obscene to be effectively enthusiastic. We can cheer and taunt with style; that should be the Duke trademark. Crudeness, profanity, and cheapness should not be our reputation—but it is.

The last subject to discuss is physical appearance for a game. The Crazies are known not only for their wild antics, but also their crazy costumes. Of these, the most notable is body painting, which I will briefly discuss here. I have a few recommendations. The mild-mannered Crazie may only paint his face, which is an acceptable tactic for one not wishing to exert excessive efforts. Nevertheless, it can be complicated. I recommend asking a friend to help you, for I've seen a botched painted face numerous times. A freshman tries to paint a "D" across his face, and not realizing that people will be looking at him, he writes it backwards. For the more enthusiastic fan, full body painting is a standard. Paint selection here is important. Some people prefer to use silicon-based house paint. This works well, peels off, and doesn't rub off as easily on other people. However, I'm not much for covering my skin in potentially toxic materials, so the silicon-based paint isn't for me. If you follow my lead and use the water-based stuff, remember that it tends to come off when you sweat. Be considerate of the people around you. You don't want to smear their clothes, often white Duke t-shirts, with blue paint from your sweating body.

Otherwise, be creative. See if you can devise an outfit that mocks the opposing team. For example, when Roy Williams made his first trip to Cameron after leaving Kansas for Carolina, a group of students sported *Wizard of Oz* costumes and began to chant "There's no place like home." And I bet he wanted to return home after his second consecutive defeat to the Blue Devils in his special new post coaching the Tar Holes.

If I may, let me add one last word about mental preparations. One thing the Crazies have to deal with that other fans don't is expectation. We go into every season with a target on our backs; we enter every home game with opponents coming into Cameron and gearing up to just brush off our best shots at them. Don't let the hype distract you from your game-plan and don't listen to what the media has to say about the Crazies. The national polls are always going to rank us at the top, but we can't just accept that ranking and then get lazy. We have to earn our prominence each year or else the imitators from other schools will supplant us at the top.

With my advice, you'll be ready for basketball in Cameron. If you follow this basic regimen throughout the off-season, come game time you'll be an exemplary Cameron Crazie, with enough stamina, volume, and creativity to lead the cheers. Hopefully it will rub off on the other people in your area. Remember, although we can't all be the star member of the basketball team, as the Cameron Crazies we still have an important effect on every game. And just like the players, we need to be at our physical and mental peaks.

THE PRE-LAW STUDENT

The Math Major's story inspired laughter from every
tenter. Although he was obviously joking, the actions
he described still characterized the Cameron Crazies
perfectly. I remember the Sociology Major's reply most clearly;
he loudly blurted out, "Well, I sure have the pizza-eating skill
mastered!" Almost everyone agreed that they too were all too
acquainted with the K-ville staple diet of pizza. In all honesty,
my eating habits are no exception.

The jokes and laughter continued for a while until the Pre-
Law Major drew all of the attention to herself. She had tried
several times to launch into her tale, but our Host had conve-
niently been able to quiet her down. But at last, we were coming
to the end of the game, and she would have to get her story in
before the night was over. "Now we've two stories left to hear,"
she said, "and if no one minds, I'd like to go next."

The Host looked at her, smiled and said, "By all means.
Frankly, I'm surprised you didn't speak up sooner."

The Pre-Law Student and religion major claimed angrily,
"I've tried, but you wouldn't let me!"

"I'm sorry. I must have missed you earlier," replied our Host. He tried in vain to stifle his grin. He looked quite amused, and the Pre-Law student watched him with her eyes and lips narrowed in anger. The other tenters could not keep silent as a wave of laughter rippled through the tent.

Our Host took a series of deep breaths, careful not to join in the laughter, then motioned with his arms for the tenters to settle themselves. "Anyway," he continued, "the floor is now yours. Please, tell us your story."

"I will," she retorted indignantly. She raised herself onto her knees so that she was taller than the others in the tent, all of whom were seated. Her eyes darted across the company, and her gaze fell on anyone still talking—or laughing—until the tent had gone completely silent. Once she was confident that all attention was focused on her, she began her introduction.

"In the previous tale, our friend alluded to the now-famous letter that forever changed the behavior of the Crazies. The well-known 'Avuncular Letter' to the Crazies from Uncle Terry was the trigger that motivated Duke students to replace vulgarity in their cheers with greater creativity, a reminder of the original purpose of having sports programs at this school. It is with this original purpose that I'll begin.

"Despite the neogothic chapel that towers above every other building on our campus, most people don't give too much thought to Duke University's roots as a Methodist affiliated school. John Wesley, the founder of Methodism, is the central figure in the sculpture over the archway of the chapel—and for good reason. Nor is it coincidence that our motto is *Eruditio et Religio* (that's 'Education and Religion,' for those of you who aren't Latinists). More importantly, nowhere in our religious or academic histories will we find any references to athletics.

"The great irony of our obsession with basketball is the motive for introducing intercollegiate athletics to our school. President John Franklin Crowell of Trinity College, the predecessor to Duke University, brought to the southern Methodist school the tradition of athletics he had learned during his education at Yale. In the more fashionable Northeast, athletics were becoming a significant component of instruction, as academia began incorporating more than the traditional value of educating the mind; they began the practice of educating the body as well.

"In the South, a new focus on the body came into the public consciousness after the Civil War. No longer was it sufficient for a student to be intellectually adept; he also had to be physically fit. When Crowell made athletics a part of the Trinity College curriculum, he did so as a proponent of what was known as 'muscular Christianity,' or a belief that what was good for the body was also good for the soul. By fine-tuning his physical form, a man made his body a better house for his soul. The lessons thought to be learned in either watching or taking part in athletic competition included self-discipline, sacrifice, loyalty, and motivation. These four components were also keystones in the belief of what made a good Christian.

"When they introduced athletics into the curriculum, the founders of Trinity College and Duke University could never have imagined that sports and religion would diverge so dramatically. Of the two, religion and sport, there is no question which has remained the dominant influence on the spirit of the campus. Proponents of the theory that original Christian ideals are embodied by athleticism would cringe today to see students take a Sunday morning tent shift instead of attending a church service. As fans, we violate every aspect of the athletic program that those founding religious leaders valued.

"The lewd event that inspired President Sanford's letter to the Crazies came approximately a century after athletics had been introduced at this school to promote Christian character. The year was 1984, when the unique reputation of Duke's student fans was introduced to a national audience. The Maryland Terrapins were in town for a game in Cameron. Herman Veal, then a starter for the Terps, had recently been accused of sexual assault. To make his stay in Durham a memorable experience, when Veal was introduced, the students welcomed him to the court with a barrage of condoms and panties tossed onto the floor. Throughout the rest of the game the Crazies held signs and shouted taunts hardly appropriate even for mature audiences. Indeed, athletics at Duke had reached the antithesis of their original purpose at the school.

"Journalists responded to the antics with articles scorning the behavior of Duke students. They were called everything from classless, to obnoxious, to smartasses. Yet, the media was now enamored with the Cameron Crazies . . . those loveable if sometimes crude fans that have been known to score outrageously high on their SATs and, as this reporter has even said tonight, are the future doctors and lawyers of America. But come game time, they paint their entire bodies in blue, put on fright wigs or skull caps, and yell everything from obscenities to sarcastic 'praise' at the opposing team.

"Now that I've given you some background for the original intention of having basketball on Duke's campus, you'll be able to better understand the story I'm about to tell."

"Wait a minute," interrupted the Sociology Major, "you mean that wasn't your story? Do you think we have all night?"

"No," said the religion major, "That was just my introduction. But trust me, it will help you to better appreciate my tale..."

HERE FOLLOWS THE PRE-LAW
STUDENT'S RELIGIOUS TALE

Duke Chapel's fifty-bell carillon sang high above West Campus early Sunday morning, signaling to the students, at least those few who were awake, the start of services. A late-February wind played with the stray blonde strands of Mary's hair as she climbed the few steps leading to the chapel's heavy oak doors. She glanced up at the figure of John Wesley sculpted in relief above the arched entryway and was reminded of the university's Methodist heritage.

Mary paused in the narthex, the bells now ringing directly above her head. She combed her fingers through her hair, hoping to calm the wild tresses after her walk across campus that windy morning. "I shouldn't have stayed out so late last night," thought Mary as she swallowed a long gasp of air. She exhaled, helping her shoulders to relax. The carillon released its final breath as well, signaling to Mary that services were about to begin. She ascended the stairs in front of her and passed into the nave, accepting a leaflet of hymns from the usher.

Just as they had done the first time Mary stepped into Duke Chapel on a campus tour three years earlier, her eyes darted to every corner of the neogothic church, trying to take in the entire structure in one glance—an impossible task. Had it been possible for her eyes to absorb simultaneously each aspect of the chapel, her heart would probably not have withstood the magnificence of the sight. Despite two years of attending Sunday services, Mary never tired of gazing at the Chapel's elegant arches, windows, and carvings. She wondered, How can students walk by this building every day without so much as looking up?

As she approached her usual seat in the third-to-last pew, Mary looked toward the Great Chancel Window of stained glass at the church's rear. Her eyes passed over the depictions of prominent biblical characters, ranging from Old Testament figures such as the prophets Daniel and Hosea to New Testament apostles like Philip and Matthew. She paused longest at the top of the window where the glass was said to depict the face of God as a reminder of His presence in worship.

Before sitting, Mary turned her head to the entrance of the nave and gazed at the elegant pipes of the Flentrop organ towering high on the oak gallery behind the congregation. The silver pipes glinted with shades of blues and reds from the violet light entering the chapel through the stained-glass windows.

Mary had grown accustomed to the discomfort brought on by sitting on the cold wooden benches. The soreness no longer helped her to focus on the words of the pastor, and today she thought that it might not even help her stay awake. But out walked the pastor, dressed in traditional black, to begin the service despite Mary's waning attention.

The service commenced. Mary followed the ritual mechanically. She whispered along with the choir as they sang their traditional hymns. Biblical passages were read, dotted by responses of *amen* from the congregation. She stood up. She was told to be seated. She was asked to rise again. The service progressed in this manner, just as it had a thousand times at almost every church Mary had attended since her childhood.

As the program moved toward its closing, the pastor began his sermon. Today, he opened with a quote from Shakespeare. The black-cloaked arms of the portly minister leaned heavily on the wooden lectern. The register of his voice fell into a low octave as he filled the echoing nave with the warning, "O, beware, my lord, of jealousy! It is the green-eyed monster which doth mock the meat it feeds on." What followed was a sermon alluding to the story of the brothers Cain and Abel, and how Cain, jealous of the seeming favor God showed toward his brother, murdered Abel and tried to hide it from the Holy Father.

Mary was awakened from a reverie by the sounds of closing

books and the whispers of nearby congregation members that signaled to her the end of services. The sumptuous chords of the organ drifted overhead into the hollows of the nave as the half-filled church emptied onto the chapel's front lawn.

As she exited from the narthex, passing once again through the heavy doors of the portal, the morning's low sun forced Mary to squint. The chapel carillon tolled its joyous song to the westerly wind from two hundred feet above, signaling to the still-quiet campus that the Sunday morning service had ended. Never tiring of the grandeur and elegance of the Chapel's commanding presence on campus, Mary looked once more toward the top of the chapel. From her close proximity to the base, the four spires of the chapel tower seemed to pierce the wispy clouds of the otherwise blue heavens.

The wind pushed Mary's hair once again across her face and into her eyes. She brushed the stray strands aside as she lowered her head and turned from the chapel. Then Mary walked away from that Canterbury-inspired tower, and began her pilgrimage toward the hollowed halls of another campus shrine, Cameron Indoor Stadium.

Mary stopped by her room long enough to hang up her Sunday dress and replace it with a pair of jeans and a Duke t-shirt. She pulled her hair into a ponytail, picked up her backpack, put on a windbreaker, and went to meet her friends in line outside of the stadium.

"Thanks for holding a spot for me," said Mary as she found the three companions with whom she always attended games, and took a seat in the extra folding chair they had set up for her on the sidewalk running parallel to K-ville. "This doesn't look too bad. What would you say, a hundred people in front of us?"

"More or less," answered her friend Peter. "We got here as soon as we could, but you know it's hard to wake up early on a Sunday morning."

"Not for Mary," responded Elizabeth. "Since she's been my roommate, I haven't seen her sleep in and miss church once."

"Whatever makes her happy," said Paul. He extended his arms in a gesture of revelation, hands open, palms up, and explained, "As for me, I can do all the worshiping I need right here." With their eyes, the four friends looked in the direction of Paul's gesture, the sprawling tent city erected across the lawn in front of them.

The Crazies still had four hours of waiting until the doors would open for Duke's Sunday evening game against Virginia. In the meantime, Peter had a newspaper folded to the sports page. Elizabeth and Paul had moved their chairs next to each other and were sharing the screen of a laptop. Mary pulled out her own computer and opened the screen. "Oh, you brought your laptop too," said Paul. "Good. You can help us dig up information about the Virginia players."

"No problem," answered Mary as she clicked the icon to enable her wireless card and access the network. "But first, I have to take a look at the articles on Duke Basketball Report. I haven't checked it since last night."

"There's a funny story about a new UNC recruit that you've

got to read," said Peter from behind his paper. "Something about him being the savior of the Carolina program."

"That's only if he doesn't jump straight to the NBA like their last three big recruits," responded Mary. And in similar conversation, the hours before the game were wiled away by basketball discussion until about thirty minutes before the doors were scheduled to open.

The line had now grown to the back of K-ville, coming to an end near the IM Building. "I guess we better get ready for the game," suggested Elizabeth as she snapped closed the lid of her laptop.

"I can take this stuff to the tent," said Paul, gathering the chairs and bags. "I'll be right back."

"Don't forget the game stuff," called Mary as Paul disappeared into the maze of tents.

Two minutes later Paul returned to the line toting two plastic grocery bags. He set them on the ground and said, "Let the pregame sacraments begin."

The four friends started their ritual by painting their faces. After everyone had smeared blue across their foreheads, cheeks, noses, and chins, Mary removed the bottle of white from the bag and said, "I'll do the letters." She approached Peter first. Much taller than Mary, he was forced to bow his head as she proclaimed, "You will bear the mark of the *D*." Elizabeth received the *U*, Paul the *K*, and finally, Mary the *E*.

The second of the two bags contained a pair of wigs. Peter fixed the blue one to his head while Paul took the white. Also in the bag were two pairs of novelty plastic horns: one for Elizabeth, and the other for Mary. When she had finished tying the strap to hold the horns in place, Mary turned to Peter and said, "Well, do I look like a Blue Devil?"

The students flashed their student ID cards to four separate line monitors and security officials outside of Cameron. Then they arrived at the entrance, where a fifth person, another line monitor, was charged with swiping the IDs through the card readers at the door. Mary handed him her DukeCard and he slid the magnetic strip on its back through the machine. A high-pitched beep told him that her card was valid.

Mary passed through the heavy oak doors of Cameron Indoor Stadium. She could hear a song from the Duke pep band playing in the arena. Mary paused in the narthex of the stadium to adjust the novelty horns affixed to her head. She took a long breath, smelling the popcorn and pizza from the nearby concession stand. When she dropped her shoulders, and released the air, out came a quiet phrase, "Let's go devils."

Once the four friends had entered the stadium, they raced toward the TV side. Mary paused a moment to take a pamphlet of suggested cheers and facts about the opposing team from the hand of a nearby line monitor. Ignoring pleas from the stadium officials to slow down, Peter, whose face bore the D, stepped onto the wooden bleachers first, followed next by Elizabeth with her U, Paul with his K, and Mary with her E.

Just as they had done the first time Mary stepped into Cameron on a campus tour three years earlier, her eyes darted to every corner of the neogothic arena, trying to take in the entire structure in one glance—an impossible task. Had it been possible for her eyes to absorb simultaneously each aspect of the stadium, her heart would probably not have withstood the magnificence of the sight. Despite two years of attending games, Mary never tired of gazing at the stadium. Modern arenas are unlikely to sport elegant wood paneling and brass railings or to allow spectators to be so near the court that they can touch the players. But Cameron's age affords it these advantages.

As she and her friends dashed toward a bench three rows from the front, Mary looked toward the rafters above the graduate student section. Hanging from the iron beams were banners representing the players with retired jerseys. Her eyes passed over the numbers of prominent figures in the history of Duke basketball, ranging from Dick Groat and Mike Gminski in the days before Coach K, to the new era of Duke basketball that ushered in such players as Grant Hill and Jason Williams.

Before facing the court, Mary turned and looked at the end of the stadium opposite from the hanging jerseys. Above the entrance to the arena she had come through hung three banners signifying Duke's national championships from 1991, 1992, and 2001. The white banners shone brightly in spotlights that hung above to keep them always illuminated.

Mary could feel the uncomfortable sting return to her calves as she took her stance on the bench. However, having to stand on the cold, wooden bleachers for hours every game had allowed her to grow accustomed to the ache. The pain seemed insignificant. It now served more as a reminder of sacrifice than as punishment. More important, it would be forgotten as soon as the game began and her attention became focused solely on basketball.

While the players performed warm-up drills on the court, the choir of students practiced their chants. Praise in the form of synchronized "Let's Go Duke!" cheers echoed throughout the iron-arched nave of Cameron. Interspersed with the chants were motivational melodies from the band. Over the course of the next hour, as the earliest-arriving fans cheered their players, and taunted the opponents, the remainder of the Cameron congregation filed in. By game time, hardly a space could be found in the student section or the upper seats.

With only moments left before the opening tip, Coach K entered the arena wearing a black suit and tie. As he strode across the court named in his honor, the student fans began their customary half-bows in honor of their basketball deity.

When the clock had run out, the horn sounded and the traditional basketball "service" began. The teams stepped off the court and stood at their respective benches. The national anthem was played and the players were announced. Coach K kneeled on one knee before the Duke bench and made the sign of the cross on his chest. The referee, the high priest with authority over the ceremony, began the game by launching the sacred object into the air. The orange leather orb was tipped away from center court and into the hands of a waiting Duke player.

The first of the chorus's spiritual chants began as Duke set its offense. Twenty seconds fell off of the clock before the first shot was sunk . . . a three pointer from the baseline. A wave of praise filled the air as students all around raised their hands to give high-fives to their neighbors.

Virginia took the ball, and the chorus dropped into a monotone drone. One of their guards threw up a quick shot, and it clanked around the rim, but somehow fell in. A whistle was heard at the same time as the ball's release. The Virginia player had been fouled. As he stepped to the free-throw line to take the extra shot, Mary read the name on the back of the jersey. The player's last name was Cain. "You Killed Abel!" she began to chant. As the students around her heard the cheer, and picked up on the rationale, they joined in.

Cain bounced the ball a couple of times before bringing it up to shoot. At the same time, the fans united in a jeer insinuating that the player had murdered his brother. Perhaps the cheer distracted him, or perhaps he ignored it. Either way, the shot bounced off the rim, and the ball fell into the waiting hands of a patient Duke player. The students initiated another traditional chorus as the Blue Devils pushed the ball up the court and prepared for another score.

The game flowed in this manner much of the night. Occasionally Duke would miss, or a Virginia shot would fall in the basket, but these two events happened less often than the Blue Devils made their shots—thus giving Duke a sizeable lead. Meanwhile, on the sidelines, Coach K preached to his Blue Devils. The choir of Crazies chanted from the bleachers, and the band played its hymns. The game was the sermon, and the main message was that Duke would win.

When forty minutes of game-time had elapsed, the final horn sounded, and the Devils were declared victorious. The teams exited the court as the band played Duke's alma mater. The students hooked arms around each other's shoulders, and swayed back and forth with the rhythm of the song. When it had ended, a final applause swept through the students, who were now piling up around the exits.

Mary stepped through the heavy oak doors of the portal, and entered the chilly February evening. She forced her eyes to open wide in order to see into the darkness of the night. In the scramble to exit the arena, Mary had gotten ahead of her three friends. She moved to the left of the flow of students to wait for them.

The pious girl, her face now smeared with faded blue and white paint, leaned against the base of the Schwartz-Butters Building, the tower that houses Coach K's office, and second in height on campus only to the Chapel. When she saw Elizabeth emerge from Cameron, she went to meet her. But, as she walked away from the building, she turned her head and glanced up toward the top of the edifice. From her position near the base of the monolith, it seemed as though the peak of the tower cut into the star-plotted heavens above Mary's head.

THE ENGLISH MAJOR

By the time the Pre-Law Student had ended her tale, the moon must have stood high in the sky. We had been telling stories for such a lengthy time that I could hardly believe the third personal check had yet to arrive. Looking down at my watch I saw that the hour was nearing two o'clock, and K-ville was quieting down despite the hordes of students all around.

"Well, guys," said the Line Monitor. "I think I'll head back outside and . . . uh . . . finish my rounds."

"Finish your rounds, huh?" the Math Major asked skeptically. "Have fun with that."

The Line Monitor walked through the circle, stepped over the Sociology Major's shoulder, and left the tent. Once his footsteps could no longer be heard, the Sociology Major jumped up and exclaimed, "Yes! They're about to call the third check!"

"How do you know?" asked the Freshman, sounding disappointed.

"It's obvious," retorted the Public Policy Major. "Why else would he leave with just one story left?"

"I'm sure they'll call the check soon," said the Captain, "but we could still have another half hour."

"Let's move along, then," said our Host, rushing us into the next tale, just as he had been doing the entire night. "Everyone, we now have to get through but one last tale. You've all followed my game well, and my supervision of this game is nearly finished—so, allow me a moment to say what a pleasure this evening has been. As I warned you upon my entrance, I had never appreciated the attention that K-ville has earned. I felt as though the relatively sudden media interest ignored the influence of the student fans before the era of expanded television coverage. But I use the past tense because this evening's events have changed my opinion. With the help of you dedicated and knowledgeable students—even those of you who have had a crude word or two to say—I understand that this tent city is as much a tradition that my fellow classmates and I helped to create as it is an experience for which future generations of scholar-fans will choose to attend Duke."

Our host expelled a hearty laugh. "Now," he said, shaking his head from side to side, "I should put my sentimentality away and get us through our game. And as we move to our last story I must admit that I do not envy our final speaker. He has a daunting task ahead of him. We've already heard twelve excellent anecdotes this evening chronicling nearly every important aspect of K-ville.

"Without further delay, let us move to our friend here who, judging by his choice of reading material, I can only assume is an English major. Are you a writer or a reader when it comes to classes? Either way, it shouldn't matter. I'm guessing your experience with Literature will help you tell an impressive tale. So tell away, for you must, because every other person has spoken up. Give us the most brilliant story you can think of, so long as it has some relationship to K-ville or Duke basketball."

The English Major at once responded, "My major is indeed English. However, you were wrong to suppose that our tales have chronicled almost every aspect of Krzyzewskiville. One hundred nights and one thousand stories would fail to entirely depict the tenting experience. These eleven musings have only suggested pieces of a complex and often indescribable interweaving of emotions and events."

"He's right," interjected the Captain. "I can think of a hundred stories we've missed tonight."

"I know what you mean," said the Sociology Major. "I can't believe nobody mentioned the personal checks before the Carolina game in 2004. ESPN brought out their mobile studio and made a *College Game Day* broadcast from K-ville. It was the first time that ESPN built their entire mobile studio for a regular season *Game Day* of NCAA basketball. Amid all the excitement, we also had the largest pillow fight in recorded history."

"The largest pillow fight in recorded history?" asked our Host.

"I remember that," said the Math Major. "We had about a thousand students hitting each other with pillows while an official from the *Guinness Book of World Records* was here to verify the record by timing us for a minute."

"It's too bad other schools have broken the record since then," added the Sociology Major. "But how can a small private school like ours compete with large public universities?"

The Public Policy Major turned toward the English Major and said, "You should tell a story about how people like Uncle Harry and his wife used to come out to K-ville on cold nights and bring the students hot chocolate."

"I remember Uncle Harry," reminisced the Host. "He used to run the Duke Stores and was always doing nice things for the students here. He was great about keeping all the popular school paraphernalia stocked on the shelves. The team could win an ACC championship and the next day commemorative t-shirts would be on sale. Mind you, this was before large corporations started to mass-produce college fan merchandise."

"Don't talk about that stuff," interrupted the Pre-Law Student. "You should talk about some of the gags that the Crazies have pulled over the years. Remember that incident with Herman Veal I included in my story? After all the media criticism directed at the students, the Crazies showed up at the game against Carolina wearing halos made of aluminum foil, and they brought a huge sign that read *A Hearty Welcome to Dean Smith*."

"And while we're on the subject of funny gags," added the Economics Major, "we can't forget about the Carolina game in

2003. When one of the Tar Holes went to the free-throw line, all the Crazies sat down except for one graduate student directly behind the basket who danced around in a blue Speedo."

"Did he miss the free throws?" asked the Freshman.

"Of course he did," answered the Econ Major. "How could anyone concentrate with something like that going on in their line of sight?"

"I don't mean to push you in a specific direction for your story," said the Host to the English Major. "But, if you don't mind, I would love to hear what Coach K talks about when he meets with all the students inside Cameron the night before a game. Since he won't let anyone but students into these meetings, including the press, I've never been able to find out what he talks about. But I've always been curious."

"And you'll just have to stay curious," said the Pre-Med Student. "Those talks are off the record, and meant only for the students."

"Instead," said the Math Major, "you should talk about the logistics in tenting. You know, the important stuff—like the best places in K-ville to pitch your tent. Or talk about what some of the occupants will do to customize a tent. One year, a tent at the front of the lawn put up a sign that said *Visitor Information*. When Dahntay Jones was on the team a tent would always be called *The Inferno* in honor of his suggestive literary name. I hated that the people from that tent would wear red to games to represent the Inferno, especially when we would play a team like Maryland. That never made much sense. Of course, you could also talk about the tents every year that erect signs with the current population of K-ville."

"You know what you could talk about," said the Women's Studies Major. "We haven't heard many tales about some of the best Duke teams, players, or games. You could give us some of those."

"Why would he want to do that?" I asked. "You're forgetting that we're supposed to be telling stories about Krzyzewskiville, not about the basketball program at Duke. If someone wants to learn those kinds of details, they can look them up on the Internet."

"As you all can plainly see," said the English Major, as our attention was once again turned to the current storyteller, "since one more narrative will hardly put us closer to any true revelations about why we tent, you'll get no story from me tonight. I have a more important endeavor. Why should I paint a picture, so to speak, when I can weave a basket? A picture provides only visual enjoyment, but with a basket, I give you a useful tool in life. So if none of you is opposed, I would much rather present a logical and compelling argument for the value of our current home. If this idea suits our competition, then please allow me to proceed. I think it more reasonable to end these wonderful stories on a moral note."

We immediately agreed to his suggestion. It did seem fitting to end with a tale of appreciation for K-ville. We also thought that the English Major, perhaps more than any other tenter, deserved our time and attention, for he had been the sole group member who could never be overheard complaining about his tenting obligations.

Our Host was our spokesman for these sentiments. "Good luck to you!" he exclaimed. "Now go ahead because we're all interested in learning the moral. But please, it's getting late, and we're fairly certain that the final check is about to arrive. Be expressive but brief, if it's not too much to beg. Now say what you like. We'll be happy to listen."

After the Host's request, the English Major began.

HERE THE ENGLISH MAJOR GIVES US OUR LAST TALE

In recent years, the Cameron Crazies have come into some criticism from journalists, television outlets, Internet message boards, and fans at other schools all trying to convince us, but mostly themselves and the public, that the Crazies aren't what they used to be. They claim that we're not as creative as the Crazies of past generations, that we're more concerned with entertaining ourselves than with getting into the heads of our opponents, that we're a bunch of nerds who are either going to basketball games or studying, and that we're merely living off of our reputation.

Listen to what those people tell you, be polite, be respectful, and then disregard whatever claim they made, because arguing with them will do you no good. A person either hates Duke or loves Duke, but changing their opinions is not something you're likely to be able to do, or perhaps even something you need to attempt. The truth is that the Cameron Crazies aren't any worse now than they were five or ten years ago, and they aren't any better either; the Cameron Crazies are perfect for the moment they're in. Back in 1986, the Crazies could be outrageous; they could pull off throwing condoms and panties at a Maryland player because of different security measures and different perceptions of what were deemed "acceptable practices" by fans. If we threw objects on the court today, we would be thrown out of the stadium, and Duke could risk forfeiting the game. Today making a gag out of a sexual assault charge would be deemed completely inappropriate.

Although the outside world might believe otherwise, the antics of the current students aren't necessarily geared at intimidating the opponent. We show up to games in order support our team, and distracting the opposing team is a secondary goal. Coach K wants us to have fun in the stands, but he doesn't want our focus to be the other players; he wants us to focus on our fellow students. When a sportswriter writes a column criticizing our effectiveness at taunting, he's telling a group of youths that they need to do a better job of insulting people. What kind of lesson is that for a generation preparing to enter the working world? That same writer will then move on to condemn us for glorifying Coach K, but at least our Coach is teaching us to be respectful and supportive.

The animosity thrown toward Duke and its students from the media and opposing fans is ridiculous. People become so invested in sports in general, and their teams in particular, that they forget the relative importance of what they're participating in. During the 2004–2005 campaign, Duke suffered from an already short bench thanks to early defections to the NBA, and to add to the team's problems, they went on to experience a series of unfortunate injuries. When asked by the media how the injuries were influencing the ability of the team to win, Coach K responded by saying, "You know, I do so much work with The V Foundation and Children's Hospital. We have some injuries, but come on, we're playing basketball. If we make excuses because of injuries, we're complete idiots, as far as what's going on around us."

Cheer for your team. Love your team. Worship your team if you must. But be certain to put your fanaticism for athletics in perspective. Basketball is still a game, and when that game is over, we need to remember that we're all people, and as such, we should be respectful to one another. Try to understand why you appreciate a sport or a team as much as you do instead of focusing on how much you hate an opposing program. I might hate Carolina's basketball team, but I'm not going to threaten a person, harm someone, or cause physical damage because of school affiliation. Some fans, however, take their athletic grudges too far. Whether it be a sportscaster who publicly denounces an entire student body because of their devotion to the school's teams, or some Maryland fans that riot after a victory or loss to

Duke, there are too many people in this world that take athletics too seriously.

I love Duke basketball, but I love it because of what the program represents, not because they have a rich tradition of winning. I use tenting as a means to help demonstrate that appreciation.

I'm often asked the question, "Why do you tent?" I daresay everyone else here has had such an encounter. It's a logical question. To an onlooker who has never experienced tenting or the student section in Cameron, Krzyzewskiville makes no sense. Why do students dedicate countless hours to their tents? "Isn't it cold out there?" these curious observers ask. "Don't you have to go to class?" Some people try to use reason to better understand K-ville. They wonder, "Why would you spend weeks at a time to get into a game of basketball that only lasts two hours?" People have gone so far as to ask if I get a discount in tuition to sleep in a tent.

"I know why I do it," is my answer. But when I try to explain, the words don't seem to be there. I'm a student immersed in language, but finding the proper answer is a task I'm unable to accomplish. Perhaps words are still too primitive a tool to explain all human actions. Instead of giving an answer a stranger to K-ville can appreciate, I'm forced to say, "If you've ever been part of the student section in Cameron, you'll understand my reasons."

We are the famed Cameron Crazies. We are basketball's greatest group of fans. Our presence inside Cameron Indoor

Stadium is part of why the stadium is the perfect environment to watch a sporting event. In no other venue will you find a more dedicated crowd. With our participation we help the team to victory, but our mistakes can cause the team to lose as well. And yet, this justification still fails to explain our enthusiasm. Instead, my response only reiterates our devotion.

Why? Why do we love Duke basketball?

Why? Why devote so much time to a game in which we have no physical role?

We've heard a number of stories, but in none of them have we found the answer. Our revelations may even have compounded the problem. Many of the tales have included complaints and concerns with the tenting experience. I imagine these critiques don't add to a desire to tent. You've all praised K-ville as well, but no one has explained his reason for tenting other than premium seating in a stadium and a love of Duke basketball. As some of you have aptly pointed out, appreciation for the team, the program and the game doesn't necessitate our need to spend months in a tent. Whether you spend four weeks in line or four hours, you can still have the same devotion to Duke basketball.

It is in our being out here tonight we've answered the question of why we tent, though not from the lessons or morals of the stories presented this evening. Being here together is why we tent. If you don't believe me, look at the people sitting around you. On your right is a friend you may have never met had it not been for this experience in the tent. On your left might be a person you knew before, but this very evening you learned something more about that fellow student and his or her thoughts and beliefs.

In several of your stories you mentioned the *Duke community*. Truly there's no place where the term is more appropriate than in describing K-ville and the games in Cameron. Remember the person who stood next to you at last week's game? Remember giving him or her a high-five after that three-pointer was made? You might not have known the person's name, but at that moment of mutual pride, you must have felt an undeniable bond that only people with similar passions can share. You had come together with more than a thousand classmates, all of whom were people representing the same choice you made.

You're at Duke! Very few people can make that claim. The basketball program is an extension of your accomplishment. You're not watching highly paid athletes, members of a professional team from your city. The kids you're cheering for are your classmates. They made the same decision you did to come here, are a representation of your school and, by extent, of you. In addition, the other Crazies, your fellow fans, are a similar picture of yourself. Although they're not all jumping around in the front row wearing a white wig and painted blue, all the fans have a similar interest — or what would they be doing waiting in a tent or screaming in the bleachers? Don't you feel that connection? It's one you'll have the rest of your life.

When you're out here, remember why. Don't think that you're simply waiting in line. You wait in line to see a movie, standing alongside strangers that may have nothing in common with you. You wait in line to sit on a plane for a few hours with a group of people you've never met, nor are you likely to see again. But in Krzyzewskiville you're part of a community that boasts a multitude of unifying characteristics. Never again will you be a member of such a community. And one day, when you're walking to class, you'll see a student who spent two months living in a tent three spots to the left of yours. Although her name might be a mystery, don't be afraid to smile. The two of you share a similar life experience. Both of you are passionate about the college decision you made. Both of you know that you couldn't have found a better world in which to live and play.

When you reflect on the time you spent in K-ville and begin to recount your stories to a future generation, you'll understand my words. You weren't sitting out here strictly as a fan. Your devotion to the game or to the team won't mean nearly as much as the student community of which you've been a vital part.

HERE WE END WITH AN EPILOGUE TO
THE ENGLISH MAJOR'S TALE

By fortune's will, those words ended the English Major's tale. Whether or not he had finished his treatise will remain a mystery, because the wail of a siren broke in without warning. The result as always, and as some tales have discussed, was the beginning of commotion, both in and around our tightly packed tent. Hundreds of students prepared themselves to embrace the cold and confusion of their personal check, and the final one for a majority of K-ville's residents.

As for Tent 25, much to the distress of both our Host and our Captain, we filed out in anything but an orderly fashion. The Captain yelled to the group as it scurried out, "Wait outside of the tent so that we can stay together and find our check point together." None of the tent members heeded his order, so he pleaded, "Please, it will be easier to make sure everyone's accounted for." But by this time, most everyone had left the tiny confines of our tent. They now had the responsibility of finding, on their own, the monitor with the checklist containing the names of the occupants of Tent 25.

The Host, much to his dismay, had not yet had the opportunity to make a ruling on the competition's winner. "Remember, after the check, come back to the tent!" screamed the Host, but no one heard him either, or if they had, they were unlikely to listen. I heard him sigh and say to the Captain, "But we haven't determined our winner." I shrugged in the direction of the two frustrated leaders and said, "At least it's stopped raining." I stepped into the icy black air.

In the end, and much to the Captain's relief, the twelve members of Tent 25 made their third and final personal check despite the chaos. As for our Host, he was disappointed. After the check, most of the group did not return to our tent in K-ville to conclude the evening's event, and as a result, the winner of our storytelling competition was never officially selected. My former tent mates and I still quarrel over whose story would have been selected. Thus, with no other option except to relate our conflicting opinions, it is probably best to entrust the decision to your preferences. What story of K-ville did you most prefer?

GENERAL EPILOGUE

HERE END THE TALES OF
KRZYZEWSKIVILLE

All the members of Tent 25 had completed three of five personal checks. But any good tenter knows that there were still two checks to come during the night; since a personal check also serves as a standard tent check, one tent representative had to be present to hold our group's spot in line, or else we would be penalized for having missed a check and would be sent to the end of the line.

Despite the importance of someone staying in the tent, the other tenters had made a fast break for the warmth of their rooms. I, on the other hand, had left my books and laptop in the tent during the commotion stirred by the tent-check siren. Before going to my room, I first had to retrieve my school bag. Once there, I met our Captain. His face was pale, and he was frantically searching for the occupants of our tent. When he saw me approach, he anxiously asked, "Why has everyone left?"— as though I needed to explain that it was both late and cold, and despite our collective excursion to K-ville, classes would indeed be in session tomorrow. "We still need someone to stay the rest of the night," he moaned. "One of us has to be accounted for in the next two checks. I would stay, but I have a test tomorrow morning and I really need some sleep. That won't happen if I have to wake up for checks in the middle of the night."

By this time, the English Major had also returned to the tent. He asked me, "Did that reporter leave my scarf?"

"Not that I'm aware of," I answered, and then pointed to the Captain. "Maybe he knows."

The English Major opened his mouth, but had yet to form a sound before our distressed Captain turned back toward us and asked, "Can either of you spend the night in the tent? I hate to ask you, but I don't see anyone else. Please do this favor for me. I'll find a way to pay you back. I'll take one of your night shifts in a couple days when tenting starts for the next big game."

The English Major, that consummate K-villite, never did ask the Captain about his scarf. Instead, he told his friend, "I don't mind staying out tonight."

Before this evening, I might have been happy to hear him accept. But I had learned something through the telling of these stories. My appreciation for K-ville and the students it represents had grown with each tale offered to me. I wasn't only tenting for admission to a basketball game, and I wasn't tenting because it was a "Duke thing" I had to do sometime during my four years at school, as so many people have often expressed. I was out here to continue a tradition which signifies the devotion, love, and community of Duke University's students.

The Captain left the English major and me standing outside Tent 25. The English Major began to untie his leather laces in order to remove his shoes before reentering the tent. But before he could undo the first knot I stopped him and said, "You can go home. I want to spend the night."

He didn't question my decision, or thank me for my offer. The English Major merely flashed me a small smile. As I bent down to untie my own shoelaces, my well-read friend offered me a sort of prize for our unfinished game. "Perhaps," he said, "the true reward in tonight's contest was not to save the victor from having to endure one of his tent shifts. Maybe the winner is in fact compensated by getting to spend more time in Krzyzew-skiville." After he spoke these words to me, the English Major passed the strap of his bag over his shoulder and across his chest. Then he turned and glided away toward West Campus.

"Wait," I called after him. He paused and turned to face me. I ran toward him with my bare feet slapping against the cold, wet cement. When I reached him, I pointed at his uncovered neck. "Take this" I offered, and proceeded to unwrap my gray cotton scarf. The first pieces of soft fabric folded into his outstretched hand before the final lengths tumbled over his fingers and hung from his palm. We stood eye to eye for a silent moment.

"Thanks," said the English Major, and then he turned away from me once more. My eyes followed his steps until night's darkness had collapsed around him. He was the last of the night's fellowship to leave, and I realized with his departure that I hadn't wanted our evening of storytelling to end.

I went back to our tent. Once inside, I pulled the zipper closed and removed my laptop from its leather case, opened the lid, and began to record the stories told this very night in order to preserve them for future judgment. And in this winter season, and upon this freezing day, I write to you from Krzyzewskiville as I lie alone in my tent, wrapped in layer upon layer of clothing and blankets, passing the time until the other students return for the game against Carolina, so that we can once again represent Duke's home-court advantage.

> My stories here do find an end, the pledge
> To write this night's events has not been failed.
> Enjoy now these Krzyzewskiville Tales.

CRAZIE TALK

A Glossary

When it's all said and done, Krzyzewskiville isn't about
a game or devotion to a team, it's about the moments you get to
spend together with friends, all sacrificing for the same goal. . . . It's
our social group coming together with 100 other social groups to be
the most intimidating home court advantage in the history
of sports. — RAY HOLLOMAN, *"A Day*
in the Life of K-ville"

S ince its inception, K-ville has become a neighborhood with a set of rules and even a body to enforce its policies, all controlled by the Duke Student Government. Over the years the language of the Cameron Crazies has developed and evolved. Thus I present to you Crazie Talk, a key to terminology employed by the Cameron Crazies. Crazie Talk includes everything from definitions of common tenting terms to information about some of Duke's staunchest basketball opponents to etymologies of Crazie slang (with the *American Heritage Dictionary of the English Language*, 4th edition — AHD4 — serving as the dictionary of reference).

ABBREVIATIONS

adj.	adjective
AHD4	*American Heritage Dictionary of the English Language,* 4th Edition
art.	definite article
bold face	cross reference
fr.	from
n	noun
perh	perhaps
pl	plural
pref	prefix
prep	preposition
prob	probably
suff	suffix
vt	transitive verb
vi	intransitive verb

Atlantic Coast Conference (ACC) *n* [fr. AHD4 *Atlantic adj.* sense 2 + *coast n* sense 1a + *conference n* sense 3; created May 8, 1953, likely fr. coastal position of all member schools] sponsoring athletic conference of **Duke University** and eleven other Eastern U.S. schools. 2001, January 10, *Chronicle,* "Eighteen Tents and Counting": "The rise of ACC basketball has not gone unnoticed in K-ville this year" [see *K-ville*].

Blue Devil [fr. WWI French fighting unit "les Diables Bleus"] 1. *n* mascot of **Duke University** 2. *n* any student or alumni of **Duke University**. 1986, *Chanticleer,* 137: "We beg to differ, ref. Dawkins is god. If you have committed a crime, the *Blue Devils* will punish you again. They will throw underwear and stereos to make their point."

blue tenting *n* [AHD4 *blue adj.* sense 1 + Crazie Talk *tenting n;* likely fr. one of the two school colors, the other being white and designating a later tenting period] early tenting period for a tenting basketball game. 2003, February 4, Morgan (HLM), *e-mail:* "If you plan on doing *blue tenting* for UMD, you must report back to K-ville on Thursday night by 8pm" [see *UMD, K-ville*]. 2003, February 3, Morgan (HLM), *e-mail:* "Only tents that participated in *blue tenting* for the UNC game will be eligible to do *blue tenting* for Maryland" [see *tent, UNC, Maryland*]

bracelet *n* [AHD4 *bracelet n* sense 2] numbered and color-coded paper band worn on the wrist ensuring entrance into a basketball game in proper order after having waited in line. 2003, February 2, Morgan (HLM), *e-mail:* "*Bracelets* will be distributed to undergraduate students who are members of registered tents and who have completed at least three (3) personal checks on the day of the game" [see *personal check, tent*]. 2003, February 2, Morgan (HLM), *e-mail:* "Tenters who have procured *bracelets* should begin lining up at least two (2) hours prior to game time, to ensure that all tents can be placed in order before the doors open" [see *tenter*]. 2003, February 2, Morgan (HLM), *e-mail*: "To pick up a *bracelet*, a student must present a valid DukeCard or other acceptable identification as outlined in the 'Tent Checks' section of this policy" [see *DukeCard*].

bullhorn *n* [AHD4 *n bullhorn*] voice-amplifying and siren-sounding device used in Krzyzewskiville to announce **tent checks**. 2003, January 30, Morgan (HLM), *e-mail*: "We'll keep going around K-ville w/ the *bullhorn* to make it as easy as possible for you to know that there is a check going on. But ultimately, it is your responsibility to make the check" [see *K-ville, check*].

bump *vt* [AHD4 *bump v tr.* sense 4a] to be placed at end of **tenting** line after missing too many **tent checks**. 1998, November 26, *News and Observer*, "Stealing a March on Forming a Line": "If a tent misses two checks, the group is *bumped* to the bottom of the game admission list" [see *tent*]. 2003, February 3, Morgan (HLM), *e-mail*: "Also, any tent that has been *bumped* to the end of the line during blue tenting must also begin during white tenting" [see *white tenting; blue tenting*]. 2003, February 3, Morgan (HLM), *e-mail*: "In addition, any tent that did blue tenting for UNC that was *bumped* to the end of the line during white tenting will NOT be eligible for blue tenting." [see *blue tenting*, UNC]

Cameron *n* [fr. *Cameron* Indoor Stadium] abbreviated reference to Cameron Indoor Stadium, basketball arena for men's and women's basketball teams at Duke University. 2003, January 28, Morgan (HLM), *e-mail*: "I just got out of a meeting with the director of sports in *Cameron*."

Cameron Crazie *n* [fr. name of *Cameron* Indoor Stadium + AHD4 *crazy n pl* with plural s clipped] Duke University student who during basketball games sits in student section of **Cameron**. 2003, March 24, *Chronicle*: "The problem [the long tenting period] creates is that it discourages the casual *Cameron Crazie* from tenting" [see *tenting*]. 2003, March 28, *Chronicle*: "Because of his persistent involvement with the team, he is described as one of Duke's most dedicated *Cameron Crazies*."

Cameron Craziness *n* [fr. *Cameron Crazie* + AHD4 *-ness suff*] a Cameron Crazie's level of enthusiasm for Duke basketball. 2000, Bradley, *2000–2001 Basketball Admissions Policy*: "An emphasis on balancing the needs of all undergraduates, regardless of the individual's level of *Cameron Craziness*."

Camping Crazies *n* [fr. AHD4 *camping vt* + Cameron *Crazies*] **tenters** more concerned with the process of **tenting** than the subsequent basketball games. 1999, January 22, *Chronicle*: "Crazie says to fellow tenters, 'Go to hell campers, go to hell!'": "What has taken the place of the Cameron Crazies are the *Camping Crazies*. These people are more concerned with the line itself than what they are in line for" [see *Cameron Crazie*].

Card Gymnasium *n* [fr. Duke alumnus Wilbur *Card*] original West Campus gymnasium of Duke University, expanded into **Wilson** Recreation Center, which runs parallel to **Krzyzewskiville**. 2000, Bradley, *2000–2001 Basketball Admissions Policy*: "With your help and support, we can have a truly special year on that patch of grass in front of *Card Gymnasium*." 2003, January 29, Morgan (HLM), *e-mail*: "If you have tickets you will be lining up in front of *Card Gymnasium*."

Cans for Carolina *n* [fr. AHD4 *can n* sense 2a + *for prep.* sense 1 + *Carolina n*] annual program created at Duke with intention of collecting canned food items to distribute to residents in need in **Durham** community. 2003, January 29, Morgan (HLM), *e-mail*: "This week marks the kick off of the '*Cans for Carolina*' campaign! The line monitor committee is pairing up with the Durham Food Bank in an effort to collect

1000 non-perishable goods by the Carolina game" [see *line monitor, Carolina*].

Carolina *n* [fr. University of North *Carolina*, AHD4 *Carolina n*] abbreviated reference to UNC, **Chapel Hill**. 2003, January 24, Morgan (HLM), *e-mail*: "I still haven't received any t-shirt design entries. We'd like to have the shirts done and printed before the *Carolina* game." 1986, *Chanticleer*, 137: "Go to hell, Carolina."

chant sheet *n* [AHD4 *chant n* sense 2 + *sheet n* sense 2a] list distributed to **Cameron Crazies** which includes specific cheers for an upcoming game and informs Crazies of material suitable for taunting the opposing team. 2003, February 1, Corey, *e-mail*: "Anyways, whatever chants you are able to come up with, email them to me. My fellow tenters and I are going to put together a *chant sheet* and guide to distribute to everyone before game time so we can have some coordination and all be on the same page" [see *tenters*].

check *n* [fr. tent *check*] abbreviated reference to a **tent check**. 2003, January 26, Morgan (HLM), *e-mail*: "A line monitor will come out to do a *check* and call grace" [see *line monitor, grace*]. 2003, January 22, *e-mail*: "[Jeremy Morgan] has said both on this list and at a *check* that you are NOT getting grace for rush events."

cheer sheet *n* [fr. AHD4 *cheer n* sense 3b + *sheet n* sense 2a] see **chant sheet**. Bradley, "Confessions of a Cameron Crazy": "But it's not enough to rattle opponents with our outfits — we need to voice our opinions. Some fans research opposing team's weaknesses, handing out *cheer sheets* complete with heckling suggestions. And we always start badgering the visitors during warmups — no sense letting them feel comfortable in our house for a second" [see *our house*].

Chronicle *n* [AHD4 *chronicle n* sense 2] daily newspaper at Duke University. 2003, January 22, Tom, *e-mail*: "You can't be in DSG and FSAE

[Formula Society of Automotive Engineers], write for the *Chronicle*, lead an anti-war movement, triple-major in Chem, Econ, and Computer Science, work at the bookstore, volunteer at the hospital, and tent all at the same time" [see DSG, *tent*].

Clemson *n* [fr. *Clemson*, South Carolina] **Atlantic Coast Conference**-affiliated school located in Clemson, South Carolina. 2003, February 7, Morgan (HLM), *e-mail*: "Finally, the Clemson game is this Sunday evening at 6:30pm." 2003, February 7, Morgan (HLM), *e-mail*: "Duke Auxiliary Services has been kind enough to provide 500 free T-shirts to be distributed to the first people in line for the Clemson game."

Coach G *n* [fr. *Coach* Goestenkors + similar pattern of reference to Coach Krzyzewski] abbreviated reference to coach Gail Goestenkors, the head coach for the Duke women's basketball team. 2003, January 29, Morgan (HLM), *e-mail*: "I wanted to let you know that tomorrow (Thursday) afternoon from approximately 3:00–4:00pm there will be a pep rally for the women's team. *Coach G* will come out and speak along with a few of the women players" [see *women*]. 2003, January 31, Morgan (HLM), *e-mail*: "*Coach G* will be providing pizza for people in K-ville tomorrow afternoon at 2" [see *pizza*, *K-ville*].

Coach K *n* [*Coach Krzyzewski*] abbreviated reference to coach Mike Krzyzewski, head coach for Duke men's basketball team. 2003, February 17, Morgan (HLM), *e-mail*: "*Coach K* will be speaking in Cameron at 8pm" [see *Cameron*]. 2003, February 4, Morgan (HLM), *e-mail*: "10:00 pm — *Coach K* speech and Pep rally."

Coach K Court *n* [fr. *Coach Krzyzewski* + AHD4 *court n* sense 4] basketball court in **Cameron**. 2003, March 7, *Chronicle*, "Game Commentary": "In many ways, it was a storybook ending to Duke's home season. It was senior night in Cameron Indoor Stadium, a night for adoration to pour down on Andre Buckner, Dahntay Jones, and Casey Sanders in their final game on *Coach K Court*" [see *senior night, Cameron*].

Crazie Talk *n* [fr. Cameron *Crazie* + AHD4 *talk n* sense 6] slang or jargon of the Cameron Crazies.

Crazy Towel Guy *n* [fr. AHD4 *crazy n* sense 2a + *towel n* + *guy n* sense 1] nickname given to Herb Neubauer, a Duke alumnus who attends almost every Duke home basketball game (as well as other Duke sporting events), sitting in section 7, row G, seat 8. He is specifically recognized for standing and whipping a towel around in circles over his head and pumping his fist with the other hand in the upper seats of **Cameron** Indoor Stadium. 2003, January 21, Vivion, *e-mail*: "Really none of us is hard-core. *Crazy Towel Guy* is hard-core" [see *hard-core*].

Devils *n pl* [fr. Blue *Devils*] abbreviated reference to the title of **Blue Devils**, the Duke University mascot. 2003, February 1, *e-mail*: "It was an amazing game, we played with heart, and I'm truly sorry that not everybody could be in there to feel how great it was. Way to rock, *Devils!*" 1986, *Chanticleer*, 137 "The ball orange as fire falls more times for the *Devils* in Cameron than for anyone else" [see *Cameron*].

DSG *n* [fr. *Duke Student Government*] acronym for Duke Student Government, the elected student governing organization and administrative organization for **Krzyzewskiville** and the **line monitors**. 2003, January 24, Morgan (HLM), *e-mail*: "If you are interested, be sure to get your entry into the DSG office ASAP!" 2003, February 7, Morgan (HLM), *e-mail*: "DSG will be sponsoring two bands on Sunday afternoon."

Duke *n* [fr. *Duke* University] abbreviated reference to Duke University. 2003, January 22, LaFerney, *e-mail*: "The way it is now, hard-core *Duke* basketball fans are penalized for being involved in too many activities" [see *hard-core*].

Duke Basketball Report *n* [fr. *Duke* University + AHD4 *basketball n* sense 1 + *report n* sense 4] website celebrating all things related to Duke basketball. 2003, January 30, Morgan (HLM), *e-mail*: "If you guys aren't already aware, there is a website completely devoted to Duke Basketball . . . www.dukebasketballreport.com. Affectionately, it is known as DBR."

Duke blue *n* [fr. *Duke* University + AHD4 *blue* n sense 1] navy blue, one of the two school colors of Duke University, the other being white. 1986, *Chanticleer*, 137: "That is, except for those dribbling balls dressed in basketball garb of a color other than *Duke blue.*"

DukeCard *n* [fr. *Duke* University + AHD4 *card n* sense 1d] student ID issued by Duke University for identification verification purposes. 2003, January 28, Morgan (HLM), *e-mail*: "They will ask you to leave either your driver's licence or *DukeCard* with them while you have the laptop checked out" [see *laptop*].

Duke University *n* [fr. Washington *Duke* + AHD4 *university n* sense 1] private university located in **Durham**, North Carolina. Originally named Trinity College until James B. Duke endowed the school in 1924 and had its name changed in honor of his father, Washington Duke. 2001, King, *Duke University: A Brief Narrative History*: "President Few urged that the school be called *Duke University* since the name Trinity College was not unique."

Durham *n* [fr. Dr. Bartlett Snipes *Durham*] city in north-central North Carolina with a population of approximately 195,800; home city of Duke University and **Krzyzewskiville**.

effective order *n* [fr. AHD4 *effective adj.* sense 3 + *order n* sense 4] proper numerical order of **tents** in line when accounting for **bumped** tents 2003 Jan 26 Morgan *e-mail*: "Later tonight I will send out an e-mail letting you know the *effective order* of the tents in the line."

effective tent number *n* [fr. AHD4 *effective adj.* sense 3 + *tent n* sense 1 + *number n* sense 1a] actual **tent number** taking into consideration **bumped** tents in the line. 2003, January 26, Morgan (HLM), *e-mail*: "Before I added all of the new people to the e-mail list, I wanted to let you know where everyone stood following blue tenting . . . Tent Number *Effective Tent Number*: 1 is 1; 2 is 2; 3 is 3; 4 is 4; 5 is 5; 7 is 6" [see *blue tenting*].

Florida State *n* [fr. *Florida State* University] **Atlantic Coast Conference**-affiliated school located in Tallahassee, Florida. 2003, March 7, *Chronicle*, "Game Commentary": "The Blue Devils jumped out to a 40–20 lead en route to an easy 72–56 victory, avenging an earlier loss to *Florida State*" [see *Blue Devils*].

game grace *n* [fr. AHD4 *game n* sense 2a + *grace n* sense 6] type of **grace** from **tenting** given during other non-tenting basketball games in order that no person tenting will miss viewing or attending other Duke men's and women's basketball games. 2003, January 31, Dinin, *e-mail*: "We just went over the tent schedule and came up with the *game graces*. . . . [F]or everyone who misses an entire shift due to a game, it would be greatly appreciated if he or she could replace that shift on that particular week with one of the empty shifts for that week" [see *tent, shift*].

Georgia Tech *n* [fr. *Georgia* Institute of *Tech*nology] **Atlantic Coast Conference**-affiliated school located in Atlanta, Georgia. 2003, January 23, Morgan (HLM), *Chronicle*, editorial: "This Saturday, the men's basketball team will face off against *Georgia Tech* at noon in Cameron Indoor Stadium" [see *Cameron*].

grace *n* [AHD4 *grace n* sense 6] temporary reprieve from tenting during which no **tent checks** will be called and no member of a **tent** must be present in **Krzyzewskiville**. 2003, February 10, Teel, "Cameron: Part of Us": "This is a '*grace*' period, a time when the Crazies' presence is not required. There are *grace* periods for class, sporting events, and sub-zero temperatures" [see *Cameron Crazies*]. 2003, January 23, Morgan (HLM), *e-mail*: "I wanted to drop everyone a line to let you know that *grace* will end tomorrow (Friday) at noon. Make sure at least one member of your tent is present at that time."

hard-core *adj* [AHD4 *hardcore adj.* sense 1] describing an extremely dedicated fan, often used to describe the **Cameron Crazies**. 2003, January 22, Tom, *e-mail*: "You are not truly *'hard-core'* if you consider other options than your tent" [see *tent*]. 2003, January 22, Dan, *e-mail*: "The way it is now, *hard-core* Duke basketball fans are being penalized for being involved in too many activities."

head line monitor (HLM) *n* [AHD4 *head adj.* sense 2 + *line n* sense 18 + *monitor n* sense 1] **line monitor** in charge of all other line monitors who oversees entire **tenting** process as an agent of DSG. 2001, February 1, Sarowitz, *The First Krzyzewskiville*: "Krzyzewskiville has become a complex community with rules and policy that are pages long. The 'boss' of Krzyzewskiville, the *head line monitor*, even holds a cabinet-level position in Duke Student Government" [see *Krzyzewskiville*]. 2003, January 21, Vivion, *e-mail*: "If we all were really hardcore we would be sleeping there despite the cold, we would not be having this discussion, Nan would be the *head line monitor* instead of Jeremy Morgan" [see *Jeremy Morgan*].

horn *n* [fr. bullhorn] abbreviated reference to the **bullhorn** used in **Krzyzewskiville** to announce **tent checks**. 2003, January 30, Morgan (HLM), *e-mail*: "After nearly every check, I've received two or three e-mails from people complaining that they missed their check because they didn't hear the *horn*" [see *check*]. 2003, January 30, Morgan (HLM), *e-mail*: "Second, the line monitors have all been instructed repeatedly to go around K-ville with the *horn*" [see *line monitor, K-ville*].

integrity of the line n [fr. AHD4 *integrity* n sense 2 + *of prep.* sense 8 + *the art.* sense 1 + *line* n sense 18] the order and positioning of students in line according to the proper **tenting** guidelines established by DSG. 2000, Bradley, *Undergraduate Admissions Policy for the 2000–2001 Men's Basketball Season*: "The Head Line Monitor will make a concerted attempt to have a sufficient line monitor presence to protect the *integrity of the line* any time students are waiting for a game" [see *head line monitor, line monitor*].

Krzyzewskiville n [fr. Mike *Krzyzewski* + AHD4 *-ville suff*; first used in 1986 to describe first group of tents outside Cameron Indoor Stadium] **tent** city at Duke University where students wait in line for entrance into basketball games in **Cameron**. 2003, January 20, Morgan (HLM), *e-mail*: "This is an e-mail group for all members of the tent city at Duke University known as *Krzyzewskiville*."

Krzyzewskiville Plaza n [fr. *Krzyzewskiville* + AHD4 *plaza* n sense 1] rectangular plot of grass on which the **Krzyzewskiville tents** are erected. 2000, Bradley, *Undergraduate Admissions Policy for the 2000–2001 Men's Basketball Season*: "Generally, [the queue] will start adjacent to the East side of Cameron Indoor Stadium (the student entrance) proceed South next to Card Gymnasium, the Wilson Recreation Center and *Krzyzewskiville Plaza*." [see *Cameron Indoor Stadium, Card Gymnasium, Wilson Recreation Center*]. 2000, Bradley, *Undergraduate Admissions Policy for the 2000–2001 Men's Basketball Season*: "Krzyzewskiville will officially open when there are ten (10) affiliated groups with tents erected in *Krzyzewskiville Plaza*" [see *Krzyzewskiville*].

K-ville n [fr. *Krzyzewskiville*] abbreviated and more easily spelled title of **Krzyzewskiville**. 2003, January 30, Morgan (HLM), *e-mail*: "Also, I would highly recommend that you send a representative or two out to *K-ville* to take a look at your tent" [see *tent*]. 2003, January 21, Vivion, *e-mail*: "*K-ville* is all about fun. If *K-ville* sucked then there would most definitely not be that many people out there. We all simply want to see some intense Duke basketball. Tenting is the means to that end."

K-villite *n* [fr. *K-ville* + AHD4 *-ite suff* sense 1] citizen of the **Krzyzewski-ville tent** community 2003, January 22, Noah, *e-mail*: "Hey *K-villites*, I agree with everyone else who has stated an opinion on this issue. . . . 2 AM would certainly be much easier to deal with."

laptop *n* [AHD4 *laptop n*] portable computer and important tool for doing homework while in **Krzyzewskiville**. 2003, January 28, Morgan (HLM), *e-mail*: "The library currently has *laptops* available for reserve checkout. . . . They have a battery life of 6 hours, so you should be able to use them to get lots done in your tent. The *laptops* are fully equipped with all the programs that computers in clusters have" [see *tent*].

line monitor *n* [fr. AHD4 *line n* sense 18 + *monitor n* sense 1; first line monitors appeared in 1984] person involved in keeping organization in **tenting** process, with primary emphasis on initiating and running **tent checks**. 1998, 26 October, http://sportsillustrated.cnn.com: "*Line monitors*, the student government-appointed K-ville cops who enforce the rules, will let students set up tents no sooner than 10 days before a game" [see *K-ville*, *tent*]. 2003, January 26, Morgan (HLM), *e-mail*: "You will have grace for the Super Bowl. A *line monitor* will come to do a check and call grace" [see *grace*]. 2003, February 19, Morgan (HLM), *e-mail*: "If you haven't picked up your wristband yet, the *line monitors* on duty for the walk-up line should have them" [see *wristband*, *walk-up line*].

Maryland *n* [AHD4 *Maryland n*] **Atlantic Coast Conference**–affiliated school located in College Park, Maryland, and recently, a team for which one of the two **tenting** periods is initiated. 2003, February 3, Morgan (HLM), *e-mail*: "Many people have been asking how blue tenting will work for the *Maryland* game. . . . Only tents that participated in blue tenting for the UNC game will be eligible to do blue tenting for *Maryland*" [see *blue tenting, tent*].

NCAA *n* [fr. National Collegiate Athletic Association] acronym for the National Collegiate Athletic Association, a governing sports organization of which Duke University is a member. 2003, January 30, Morgan (HLM), *e-mail*: "There are message boards to chat about everything related to Duke basketball and NCAA basketball in general."

NC State *n* [fr. North Carolina *State* University] **Atlantic Coast Conference**–affiliated school located in Raleigh, North Carolina. 2003, March 17, *Chronicle*, "Leading the Pack to Win 5 in a Row": "With 2:50 left on the clock and *N.C. State* holding a 69–68 lead over the men's basketball team, freshman J. J. Redick, a 92 percent free throw shooter, stepped to the line for a pair of attempts."

night shift *n* [fr. AHD4 *night adj.* sense 1 + *shift n* sense 2b] **tent shift** which requires a person to spend an entire night in the **tent** (generally sleeping in the tent). 2003, January 31, Dinin, *e-mail*: "The best solution we came up with is, instead of finding one person who 'has to sacrifice' their Friday or Saturday night, we should switch out those shifts per week, just like we do with *night shifts*, thus, everyone has to 'sacrifice' on weekend night if you are not already permanently signed up on a weekend *night shift*" [see *shift*].

non-TV side *n* [fr. AHD4 *non-pref.* + TV *n* + *side n* sense 7] side of **Coach K Court** which includes the player benches and television cameras, opposite the **TV side**. 2003, January 30, *e-mail*: "If at any time you find that you are not yelling something (anything . . . it really doesn't matter what), something is wrong. Start shouting . . . 'defense,' 'go devils,' the name of your favorite player/coach/opponent/hot girl on the *non-TV side* of the arena" [see *devils*].

our house *n* [fr. AHD4 *our adj.* + *house n* sense 5a] **Cameron** Indoor Stadium. Bradley, "Confessions of a Cameron Crazy": "But it's not enough to rattle opponents with our outfits — we need to voice our opinions. Some fans research opposing team's weaknesses, handing out cheer sheets complete with heckling suggestions. And we always start badgering the visitors during warmups — no sense letting them feel comfortable in *our house* for a second" [see *cheer sheet*].

personal check *n* [fr. AHD4 *personal adj.* sense 2a + Crazie Talk *check n*] specific type of **tent check**, begun two days prior to a **tenting** game, for which every member of a **tent** must be present for at least three of five. 2003, February 5, Morgan (HLM), *e-mail*: "If you haven't picked up your wristband yet and you made the 3 *personal checks*, you may go by K-ville and see any line monitor on duty" [see *wristband, K-ville, line monitor*].

pizza *n* [AHD4 *pizza n*] staple food of students in **Krzyzewskiville** and often offered free as incentive to attend an event. 2003, January 31, Morgan (HLM), *e-mail*: "Coach G will be providing *pizza* for people in K-ville tomorrow afternoon at 2. Come on out . . . should be a good time!" [see *Coach G, K-ville*]. 2003, February 6, Morgan (HLM), *e-mail*: "After his speech, Alumni Affairs will be providing *pizzas* and other giveaways to tenters" [see *tenters*].

points *n* [fr. food *points*] abbreviated reference to food points, a program by which food can be purchased with the **DukeCard**. 2003, February 7, Morgan (HLM), *e-mail*: "Bullock's BBQ will be serving food on *points* from 1pm until 2pm."

senior night *n* [fr. AHD4 *senior adj.* sense 4 + *night n* sense 1c] last home basketball game of a season during which seniors on the basketball team are honored. 2003, March 7, *Chronicle*, "Game Commentary": "In many ways, it was a storybook ending to Duke's home season. It was *senior night* in Cameron Indoor Stadium, a night for adoration to pour down on Andre Buckner, Dahntay Jones, and Casey Sanders in their final game on Coach K Court" [see *Cameron, Coach K Court*].

shift *n* [fr. tent *shift*] abbreviated reference to a tent shift. 2003, January 31, Dinin, *e-mail*: "[I]t would be greatly appreciated if he or she could replace that *shift* on that particular week with one of the empty *shifts* for that week."

sixth man *n* [fr. AHD4 *sixth adj.* + *man n* sense 2] name for entire student section, a proverbial sixth member of the five-person team on the basketball court. 1986, *Chanticleer*, 137: "Chaos reigns. The *sixth man* in Cameron has thousands of screaming heads and twice as many arms" [see *Cameron*]. 1986, *Chanticleer*, 137: "Cameron won't be quiet next year. The *sixth man* doesn't graduate."

sleeping bag *n* [AHD4 *sleeping bag n*] important tool for staying warm in the cold basketball season while sleeping in **Krzyzewskiville**. 2003, January 30, Keith, *e-mail*: "I'd recommend taking your *sleeping bag* and anything else you have in there out, unless you're sleeping there. That'll make it easier to dry the tent out, since there is definitely moisture trapped under the giant pile of *sleeping bags*" [see *tent*].

slot *n* [fr. AHD4 *slot n* sense 3a] similar to a **tent shift**; a block of time during which a specific member of a **tent** is expected to be in **Krzyzewskiville**. 2003, January 28, Donahue, *e-mail*: "Here's the latest version of the schedule. We still have a few more *slots* we need to fill, so email me back as soon as you can tell me when you can be there."

social grace *n* [fr. AHD4 *social adj.* sense 5c + *grace n* sense 6] **tenting grace** period given specifically for a social event. 2003, February 14, Morgan (HLM), *e-mail*: "*Social Grace* tonight for Valentine's Day from 6pm until 10am tomorrow morning."

student section *n* [fr. AHD4 *student n* sense 1 + *section n* sense 1] eating area of **Cameron** which consists of wooden bleachers on the stadium floor surrounding the court and which is mainly reserved for Duke student attendance only. 2003, January 31, Dre, *e-mail*: "We definitely need all the people we can get to go to the games to fill up the *student section*, but if everyone that went added something to the experience, the stadium would be jumping throughout and no one would notice any empty spaces."

swipe *vt* [AHD4 *swipe v. tr.* in sense 2] done with a **DukeCard** through card readers at the entrance to **Cameron** in order to admit authorized students into basketball games. 2003, January 26, Morgan (HLM), *e-mail*: "I plan on cross-checking my K-ville list of Unique IDs with the Duke Card Office for people that *swiped* into the game" [see *K-ville, Unique ID, DukeCard*].

tent 1a. *n* [AHD4 *tent n* in sense 1a] portable shelter, as of canvas, stretched over a supporting framework of poles with ropes and pegs, 2003, January 30, Keith, *e-mail*: "Just so you all know, the rain was like 'hey, *tent*, let me in,' and the *tent* was like 'OK,' so a lot of stuff in the *tent* is damp, and will probably be getting wetter overnight as it keeps raining." **1b.** *n* group of twelve people of which one can represent the whole during a standard **tent check**. 2003, January 22, Dan, *e-mail*: "We are forced to choose between rush events, sorority bid parties, and our *tents*." 2003, January 23, Morgan (HLM), *e-mail*: "I wanted to drop everyone a line to let you know that grace will end tomorrow (Friday) at noon. Make sure at least one member of your *tent* is present at that time" [see *grace*]. **1c.** *n* **Krzyzewskiville**, or the nearby vicinity as required by tenting bylaws. 2003, January 22, Dave, *e-mail*: "Reduce the number of people who have to be in the *tent* at 11 and then have all 8 people be there by 2." 2003, January 23, Morgan (HLM), *e-mail*: "Most likely, you will not be expected to be at your *tent* until tomorrow. Be sure to check your e-mail tonight so that you are aware of what time you need to be at your *tent* tomorrow."

tent 2a. *vi* [AHD4 *tent vi*] to camp in a tent 2b. *vi* to participate in and be a member of **Krzyzewskiville**. 2003, January 21, Tom, *e-mail*: "You can't be in DSG and FSAE [Formula Society of Automotive Engineers], write for the Chronicle, lead an anti-war movement, triple-major in Chem, Econ, and Computer Science, work at the bookstore, volunteer at the hospital, and *tent* all at the same time" [see *DSG, Chronicle*]. 2003, January 21, Vivion, *e-mail*: "I don't see how people other years could both rush and *tent*, because really Jaymo and the cold weather is the main thing that has freed us up for other activities" [see *Jaymo*].

tent check *n* [AHD4 *tent n* sense 1a + *check n* sense 4] randomized roll call, by one or more **line monitors**, of all registered tents in **Krzyzewskiville** during which a predetermined number of **tent** members must be present in order to avoid being **bumped**. 2003, January 26, Morgan (HLM), *e-mail*: "Beginning at midnight tonight with white tenting, all previously missed *tent checks* will be wiped clean" [see *white tenting*].

tenter *n* [fr. Crazie Talk *tent vi* 2b + AHD4 *-er suff* sense 1a] Person who is a member of a **tent** and subsequently involved in the tenting process in **Krzyzewskiville**. 2003, January 30, Morgan (HLM), *e-mail*: "As a *tenter* in K-ville, it's a great way to prepare for games" [see *K-ville*]. 2003, January 27, Morgan (HLM), *e-mail*: "I wanted to make you aware of an awesome program that Perkins library has going that could be very beneficial to you as a tenter."

tenting *n* [*tent vi* as in sense 2b + *-ing suff* as in AHD4 sense 1] 2003 Jan 21 Vivion *e-mail*: "We all simply want to see some intense Duke basketball. *Tenting* is the means to that end." **tenting** *adj* [*tent n* as in sense 1c + *-ing suff* as in AHD4 sense 2] describing a process involving the participation in **Krzyzewskiville** in order to be admitted into **Cameron**

for basketball games. 2003, March 24, *Chronicle*: "A six- or seven-week long *tenting* season might have been a little too long this year."

tenting holiday *n* [fr. Crazie Talk *tenting n* + AHD4 *holiday n* sense 3] Extended **grace** from **tenting** based on the completion of one period of tenting and prior to the beginning of the next period of tenting. 2003, February 4, Morgan (HLM), *e-mail*: "There will be a one night *tenting holiday* after the UNC game. If you plan on doing blue tenting for UMD, you must report back to K-ville on Thursday night by 8pm. Enjoy the night/day off" [see UNC, *blue tenting*, UMD, *K-ville*].

tent nazi *n* [*tent vi* Crazie Talk sense 2b + AHD4 *Nazi n* sense 2] **tenter** advocating strict adherence to the guidelines for **tenting** established by DSG. 2000, October 2, Bradley, "The Community of K-ville": "I've struggled with 'tent Nazis' who constantly complain that we are not 'hardcore' enough" [see *hard-core*].

tent number *n* [fr. Crazie Talk *tent n* sense 1b + AHD4 *number n* sense 4a] number which establishes a **tent**'s placement in line. 2003, February 5, Morgan (HLM), *e-mail*: "For the time being, please continue referring to your tent group with the number you were assigned at Carolina. I will give you your new *tent number* (which will be your effective tent number for this game . . . it should be on your bracelet) tomorrow" [see *Carolina*, *effective tent number*, *bracelet*].

tent sheet *n* [fr. Crazie Talk *tent n* sense 1b + AHD4 *sheet n* sense 2] checklist with names of every member of a given **tent** used in order to count the attendance of tent members at a **tent check**. 2003, January 28, Morgan (HLM), *e-mail*: "If a group wants to add somebody, simply inform the line monitor on duty during a tent check. He/she will write the person's name down on the *tent sheet*" [see *line monitor*].

tent shift *n* [fr. Crazie Talk *tent n* 1c + AHD4 *shift n* sense 2b] period of time during which a person is required to be in **Krzyzewskiville** in order to secure his or her tent's place in line in the instance that a **tent check** is called. 2003, January 30, Hussein, *e-mail*: "We will figure out the times for new *tent shifts* for white tenting tomorrow at the tent" [see *white tenting, tent*].

Towerview *n* [fr. AHD4 *tower n* sense 1 + *view n* sense 5] road running between **Cameron** and the main quadrangles of Duke University's West Campus, parallel to **Krzyzewskiville** and perpendicular to the **walk-up line.** 2003, January 29, Morgan (HLM), *e-mail*: "If you don't [have a ticket], a walk-up line will form facing Cameron going towards *Towerview.*"

TV side *n* [fr. AHD4 TV *n* + *side n* sense 7] seats on side of **Coach K Court** which are opposite the player benches and TV cameras and, as a result of television taping, is the most highly sought-after place for students to watch games. 2003, January 28, Morgan (HLM), *e-mail*: "The tickets are general admission for the TV *side* of the stadium."

UMD *n* [fr. University of Maryland] abbreviated reference to **Maryland.** 2003, February 7, Jeff, *e-mail*: "We're trying to merge with one or two white tenting groups that are interested in tenting for the UMD game. ... It means a lot to us, especially since three of us are from Maryland and have a lot of acquaintances at UMD that we'd love to shoot down" [see *white tenting*].

UNC *n* [fr. University of North Carolina] abbreviated reference to **UNC-Chapel Hill.** 2003, February 6, Morgan (HLM), *e-mail*: "Student ticket distribution for the Duke vs. UNC Women's Game Duke Undergraduate and Graduate Students can pick-up their tickets to Thursday's, February 20th #2 Duke vs. #7 North Carolina women's game TOMORROW at the following locations" [see *women*].

UNC, Chapel Hill *n* [fr. University of North Carolina at *Chapel Hill*] abbreviated reference to the University of North Carolina at Chapel

Hill, Duke University's most important rival school, games against which are always **tenting** events. 2003, February 4, *e-mail*: "Everybody come support the wrestling team tonight at 7:30 in Cameron. We wrestle UNC *Chapel Hill* and need a big crowd there" [see *Cameron*].

unique ID *n* [fr. AHD4 *unique adj.* sense 1 + ID *n*] number given to each student of Duke University which is particular to that student, in order that he or she may be identified by it. 2003, January 28, Morgan (HLM), *e-mail* "IN ADDITION, make sure that you E-MAIL ME the person's name, *Unique ID*, and e-mail address. Once I get all of that stuff from them, then the person is officially good to go as a representative for the group."

the 'Ville *n* [fr. Krzyzewskiville] Abbreviated, slang reference to **Krzyzewskiville**. 2003, January 22, Noah, *e-mail*: "Just a thought from a dedicated member of Tent 21 . . . see y'all around *the 'Ville*" [see *tent*].

Virginia *n* [fr. University of *Virginia*] **Atlantic Coast Conference**–affiliated school located in Charlottesville, Virginia. 2003, March 15, *Chronicle*, "Duke Beats Virginia, Sets Up Rematch with UNC": "The sophomore hit a three-pointer with 9:47 left to cut *Virginia's* margin to two, 14–12."

Wake Forest *n* [fr. *Wake Forest* University] **Atlantic Coast Conference**–affiliated school located in Winston-Salem, North Carolina. 2003, February 12, Morgan (HLM), *e-mail*: "We play *Wake Forest* tomorrow evening. Grace will be from 6:30pm until half an hour after the game is over" [see *grace*].

walk-up line *n* [fr. AHD4 *walk v tr* sense 1 + *up* sense 4 + *line n* sense 18] line which forms perpendicular to **Towerview**, for Duke students who did not obtain WRISTBANDS for wristband games. 2003, January 29, Morgan (HLM), *e-mail*: "If you don't [have a ticket], a *walk-up line* will form facing Cameron going towards Towerview" [see *Cameron*].

weather grace *n* [fr. AHD4 *weather n* sense 2a + *grace n* sense 6] grace extended to **Krzyzewskiville** community due to inclement weather. 2003, January 28, Morgan (HLM), *e-mail*: "Due to the snow and ice, there will be a *weather grace* until further notice."

white registration *n* [fr. AHD4 *white adj.* sense 1 + *registration n* sense 1] registration period for new **tents** to join **Krzyzewskiville** for **white tenting** 2003 Jan 25 Morgan *e-mail* "*White registration* is today at 3pm. This means that dozens more tents will be joining you in K-ville beginning this evening" [see *tent*, *K-ville*]. 2003, February 3, Morgan (HLM), *e-mail*: "All other tents may rejoin K-ville beginning this coming Sunday evening when *white registration* occurs. It will take place in the same manner as the last *white registration*."

white tenting *n* [fr. AHD4 *white adj.* sense 1 + *tenting n*; likely originating from one of the two school colors, the other being blue and designating an earlier tenting period] later, shorter period of **tenting** for tenting games which begins after **blue tenting** and requires fewer people in the **tent** at specific times. 2003, January 27, Morgan (HLM), *e-mail* "Welcome to *white tenting*. Before I added all of the new people to the e-mail list, I wanted to let you know where everyone stood following blue tenting." 2003, January 25, Morgan (HLM), *e-mail*: "Grace for Super bowl will end at midnight. At that point, *white tenting* rules will be in effect. This means that from here on out you will only need one person at your tent at all times, 24 hours per day" [see *grace*].

Wilson *n* [fr. Gary *Wilson*] one of Duke's student recreation centers, which is next to **Cameron** and runs parallel to **Krzyzewskiville**. 2003, January 28, Morgan (HLM), *e-mail*: "[A] line will form (on the sidewalk in front of *Wilson*) and the first people in that line will be the first into the stadium."

wireless *adj* [AHD4 *wireless adj* sense 1] describing **Krzyzewskiville** as

248

having Internet access requiring no wires so long as a computing device has capable equipment for such use. 2003, January 28, Morgan (HLM), *e-mail*: "Additionally, they are *wireless* ready, so you can use them to get on the Internet in K-ville (in case you weren't aware, K-ville does have *wireless* access)" [see *K-ville*].

women *n pl* [AHD4 *women n pl.* sense 2] abbreviated reference to the women's basketball team at Duke University. 2003, February 1, Morgan (HLM), *e-mail*: "Come support the *women* ... they deserve our help and without a doubt the game will be awesome." 2003, February 1, *e-mail*: "Our *Women's* Team deserves all the congratulations possible because they rocked tonight."

wristband *n* [AHD4 *wristband n*] alternate reference to **bracelet**. 2003, February 5, Morgan (HLM), *e-mail*: "If you haven't picked up your *wristband* yet and you made the 3 personal checks, you may go by K-ville and see any line monitor on duty" [see *personal checks, K-ville, line monitor*]. 2003, February 19, Morgan (HLM), *e-mail*: "If you haven't picked up your *wristband* yet, the line monitors on duty for the walk-up line should have them" [see *walk-up line*].

Library of Congress Cataloging-in-Publication Data

Dinin, Aaron.

The Krzyzewskiville tales / Aaron Dinin ; foreword

by Mickie Krzyzewski.

p. cm.

ISBN 0-8223-3633-2 (cloth : acid-free paper)

1. College students — Fiction. 2. Duke University — Fiction.

3. Basketball fans — Fiction. 4. College sports — Fiction.

5. Durham (N.C.) — Fiction. 6. Camping — Fiction.

I. Title.

PS3604.I48K79 2005   813'.6 — dc22

2005009914